AF279304

In Joppa there
was a disciple named
Tabitha (in Greek her
name is Dorcas); she was always
doing good and helping the poor.

—ACTS 9:36 (NIV)

*Ordinary Women* of the BIBLE

✦

# AN ETERNAL LOVE

## TABITHA'S STORY

### Melanie Dobson

*Ordinary Women* of the BIBLE

❖

# AN ETERNAL LOVE

## TABITHA'S STORY

Dedication

For my aunt Kathy Bowers,
who loves from the depth of her heart
and fruit of her hands

# ACKNOWLEDGMENTS

Many people encouraged and helped me as I wrote Tabitha's story. A special thank-you to my agent Natasha Kern, editor Susan Downs, and the Guideposts team for the opportunity to share this story.

Thank you to Mesu Andrews, my friend and fellow author, who answered my questions and helped me locate the references I needed.

Thank you to Michele Heath, my first reader, who asks the hard questions and always makes me dig a little deeper.

Thank you to the Bible Project for allowing me to raid their treasure trove of a resource library.

Thank you to Nicole Miller, Ann Menke, Julie Zander, April McGowan, Dawn Shipman, and Tracie Heskett—my Inklings, who graciously critiqued my work.

Thank you to Jon, Karlyn, and Kiki, whose love and mercy overflow as they follow the Way alongside me.

And a special thank-you to our Lord for the miracle of resurrection and redemption.

# Cast of
# CHARACTERS

**Biblical**

**Peter** • disciple of Jesus, apostle, and missionary to Joppa

**Simon the Tanner** • Peter's host in Joppa

**Tabitha** • disciple of Jesus, seamstress in Joppa, also known as Dorcas

**Fictional**

**Abel** • Hebrew physician

**Agathon** • ship merchant

**Bethany** • daughter of Simon the Tanner, wife of Joshua, worship leader for Joppa's church

**David** • Zoe's young son

**Diane** • wet nurse in Joppa

**Glykera** • maidservant in Tabitha's home, married to Niles

**Ianthe** • impoverished widow

**Isaac** • Tabitha's deceased husband

**Joshua** • married to Bethany, Joppa fisherman

**Korinna** • Agathon's slave

**Laurel** • a servant in Agathon's household

**Matthias** • Tabitha's adopted son

**Miriam** • widowed member of Rhapsodies

**Niles** • male servant in Tabitha's home, married to Glykera

**Selene** • Agathon's deceased wife

**Zoe** • friend of Tabitha, member of Rhapsodies

# Glossary of
# TERMS

**aloe** • precious spice used to perfume garments and bedding

**amphora** • tall jar for carrying liquids

**amulet** • piece of jewelry to ward off evil

**authepsa** • vessel used to boil water

**bier** • wooden frame to transport a corpse

**carcinos** • the crab-like threads of a tumor

**clepsydra** • ancient water clock

**colonnade** • covered walkway supported by columns

**denarius** • silver coin equal to approximately a day's wage (**denarii**, plural)

**Ekklesia** • group of Christians gathered to worship

**Elohim** • Hebrew name for Almighty God

**Hypnos** • god of sleep

**imma** • mother

**ketos** • mythological sea monster

**Leto** • goddess of motherhood

**lighter** • boat that transfers goods and passengers from a moored ship

**Lydda** • located between Jerusalem and Joppa, town where Peter heals Aeneas

**mortarium** • clay bowl used to grind spices and herbs

**nymph** • female deity of nature in Greek folklore

**parapet** • low wall along a roof

**peristyle** • columned porch encircling a courtyard

**qab** • approximate measurement, one to two liters

**rhapsode** • traveling reciter of poetry

**strigil** • clawlike tool used to scrape oil and dirt off skin

**Zeus** • king of the Greek gods

# PROLOGUE

A stone guarded her husband's tomb, the grass around it flattened from his funeral two weeks past. Hundreds had gathered to mourn the loss, but it was just Tabitha now. Alone in this quiet place.

She placed a bouquet of blue and white hyacinths beside the cavern in this olive grove, grief trickling down her cheeks. If only she could dam up her heart with a stone to stop the tears, but nothing seemed to block their flow. Sometimes her tears gushed like waves from the sea and other times they were more like the slow dripping of a water clock, marking every moment without the man she loved.

A *clepsydra*, that's what the Greek called their clocks. Water thieves.

Water had been the thief that stole Isaac from her.

Darkness was falling quickly over this olive grove, casting shadows across the knotted tree roots. Once again time had slipped away from her. She'd lingered too long outside this cavern, as if Isaac's spirit lingered with her. As if returning home meant leaving him behind.

In the distance, she heard a cry. A hyena, she guessed, come to rummage the hilltop dump nearby. At this twilit hour, she'd have to hurry back down to Joppa, to the villa that felt lonelier to her than this grove. To a city fused together by both the Jewish people and Greek.

Olive branches shuddered in the breeze, and the trees looked as if they'd been entranced by the ancient nymphs that were rumored to haunt Judea. She had no interest in mythology about nymphs or Pan—the Greek god of nature—but sometimes these trees seemed just as alive to her as her friends. Walking among them these past weeks, whispering words meant for Isaac alone, didn't stop her tears, but it calmed some of the ache in her heart.

No matter the storm that swept in from the sea, no matter the wicked heat that tormented these trees each spring, they didn't waver. Instead their roots dug deeper into the dusty soil, their arms lifting higher each year in praise to their Creator. In their worship, their branches produced the fruit that gave life to the people in her beloved city, the olive oil providing sustenance and income for their entire region.

How she wanted to be just like these trees, rooted in who God had created her to be, but her roots felt as if they were decaying in the desert winds. She felt as if she might collapse like her mother had once done long ago.

In the past year, Isaac had embraced his new identity as a follower of the Way, a disciple of a man who'd been crucified outside Jerusalem and then, according to Isaac, had walked out of His tomb three days later. The claims this Jesus made, about being both the Son of God and man, seemed heretical to her, but Isaac believed these stories. Until his death, she'd faithfully attended the meetings in Joppa with him.

Isaac had always been a good man, but he changed when he decided to follow this Messiah. Not only did he continue his work, he began to give generously of his wealth, like the rabbi named Jesus had commanded those who chose to follow Him, to offer provision to others in need.

She wanted to give of herself, like Isaac had done, but how could she give when the hollow places had seemed to expand inside her, no oil strong enough to heal the wounds of her heart? How could she serve others when she was alone and this Jesus that her husband had decided to follow seemed to steal his life away?

Now her husband's body was wrapped in linen, succumbed to the pain in this world, but if Jesus's teachings were true, Isaac's soul wasn't trapped between the folds of linen in that cave. He was worshipping in the beauty of the heavens, enjoying a palace grander than the one Emperor Tiberius had built.

God, she was certain, loved Isaac. He just didn't seem to love her.

On the other side of the grove, rancid fumes permeated the warmth of the evening, and as Tabitha stepped across a narrow stream and slipped out of the trees, the stench from the city dump burned her nose. She wrapped her black veil, the covering of grief, over her face to block the smell, but it stole right through the silk.

Usually she turned at this crossing, journeying along a path east of here instead of along this ridge, but the setting sun was a daunting opponent. She'd have to circle this dump quickly in order to make it home before nightfall.

She'd soak tonight in a rose-scented bath to cleanse the foulness from her skin, but the smell of decay, she was certain, would plague her mind much longer than her skin, and she didn't want to be reminded of its sorrow.

Life was what she needed. The welcome breeze of sea air below. The refuge of her garden lush with mint and coriander and marjoram. The villa that Isaac had built for a horde of children who never arrived.

In front of her, vapor sweated off the mount of trash at least two fathoms deep and as long as a fleet of ships. Scavengers sometimes came to the dump at this evening hour, foraging for trinkets among the rubbish, but she didn't see anyone on the hill.

Lifting the seam of her tunic, Tabitha hurried around the perimeter, her eyes focused on Joppa's villas clinging to the hillside below, their lanterns beginning to flicker with light. In the half of an hour, she would be home kneeling beside her bed, begging Adonai to reveal His love. Then she would rest her weary soul.

Another cry pierced the stillness of evening, and her body froze. Hyenas rarely bothered people, but she still didn't want to meet a pack alone at twilight.

Tabitha scanned the rugged slope, the cry growing louder, but it didn't sound like the howl of an animal. It sounded like a baby.

Voices drummed above the sound of cries, two men shouting to each other on the opposite side of the pile. They sounded desperate, as if they must find a treasure buried beneath this trash.

Either scavengers or—

Her heart seemed to stop as she slowly processed what these men might be searching for tonight, the rumors she'd heard of women leaving unwanted—damaged—babies in the dump, as if the boy or girl were garbage.

If the child survived these elements, if a slave hunter found him alive, he would be sold to…

Tabitha shook her head. She didn't want to think about what a child left in this terrible place might be forced to do.

Her hand covered her abdomen, the emptiness of her womb. And she felt the ache anew. How could any woman abandon her baby?

The two men circled to Tabitha's side of the dump, but they ignored her in their quest. Her fear of the men evolved quickly into fear for the baby hidden here.

The lights of Joppa shone brighter, a beacon at the base of this hill, but when Tabitha heard another cry, she turned away from the city, following the sound as she scaled the rotting heap.

Soggy garbage smashed under her sandals, shards of pottery scraped her ankles and toes, but she kept climbing. The men followed closely behind her, but she found the baby first, wrapped loosely in a swaddling cotton cloth, resting inside an old tub. Only hours old, it seemed.

She swept up the child—boy or girl, it didn't matter to her—ignoring the stench of soil on the cloth. The baby's cries settled into a whimper against Tabitha's shoulder.

The men were upon her now, scowling down at Tabitha as if she were a wasp burrowing into their bushel of prized figs.

The sun loomed low behind them, its crown flickering the last of its golden blaze before sinking into the sea.

In the fading light, she could see the dirt that stained the men's tunics, the tattered edges of their sleeves, beards tangled instead of trimmed. One of them stepped forward, a braided leather whip secured in his hand. "That's our baby."

Tabitha stood taller, the baby quieting as it nestled close. "Actually, *she's* my child."

While she didn't know its gender, a girl would be less valuable to slave traders than a boy.

"Why did you leave your baby in the dump?" the man demanded.

"I—" Glancing down, she saw the baby's left hand coated in soot. Few in Palestine would want to raise a child—or a slave—with a missing thumb. When the men discovered this defect, they'd probably leave it for dead. "I was going to leave her, but—I suppose I've changed my mind."

"I haven't changed mine." He stepped closer, hatred flickering in his eyes. "And I want that baby."

"It doesn't matter." Tabitha nodded toward the seaport lights. "The courts in Joppa can decide if this child belongs to me or—who are you exactly?"

The men's laughter was wicked, as if she'd made a joke. "We're merchants."

She inched back. "Merchants who know well how to buy and sell, I suppose."

"We're masters at our work."

The trader snapped his whip, and Tabitha cringed as she began backing down the messy slope, begging Adonai to keep these hunters at bay.

The whip snapped again, the tip stinging her arm, and the baby flinched, the cry from its lungs a sorrowful plea.

Anger swelled inside her as she turned back toward the men. How dare they try to hurt a baby who only wanted, *needed*, to be held. A hundred words flooded into her mind, but she dammed them up inside her lest they flood off her tongue.

If she pretended to play the hunters' game, she might still be able to rescue this child.

"Perhaps you can have her after all," she finally said.

The smile that played on the man's lips sickened her. "I'm glad you've come to understand our terms."

"Indeed." Tabitha looked down at the baby again, disdain forced upon her lips before she spoke again. "I suppose, as men who have seen the world, you would understand what to do about her condition more than I."

"What condition?"

She tilted her head, her nose crinkled. "Did you not know?"

When he didn't respond, she eased back the edge of the cotton, revealing the tiny hand of the newborn. The man with the whip stayed at the top of the pile, almost knee deep in trash, but his partner stepped down to examine the baby.

With a gasp, the man's smugness washed away like a boat in one of Joppa's storms. "Leprosy?"

The tears salting her cheeks were as real as the ones that had flowed earlier at Isaac's grave. "I want to do what's best for her."

The man backed away quickly, falling into the heap. A string of curses, longer than a dock line, sailed from his lips. Instead of threatening her again, it seemed he was terrified of this baby.

Tabitha held the child out again. "You will take her?"

Instead of replying, both men disappeared over the hump, swallowed by the darkness to their east.

Tabitha wiped away her tears with the back of her hand before turning toward the light. She cradled the baby close to her chest, hurrying back down yet taking care not to fall. If she injured herself, the two of them would have to spend the night in this abysmal mess.

She didn't know how to care for a little one, but the Messiah, in the teachings that she'd heard, made it quite clear that His followers were to love others, especially those considered to be the weakest among them. Surely someone in Joppa's community of disciples would care for this baby, even if she must pay them for their service.

When she stepped into the safety of the city, to the marketplace that had emptied itself until morning, she tore off the filthy cotton strips and scanned the baby's skin for the curse of leprosy passed along from the woman who'd birthed him.

It was a boy, this baby, and—thank God—she found no sores on his lank body. A missing thumb was merely an inconvenience, not a death sentence.

She needed to find a wet nurse this very night to care for him, lest he slip into eternity before dawn. In the morning, she would clothe him in clean linen and search for a woman—a Christ follower with other children—to mother him.

# CHAPTER ONE

Windflowers were sprinkled across the courtyard floor, the aroma of roasted lamb and peppermint settling over the guests who'd gathered to celebrate. The wedding banquet would last for days, perhaps an entire week, depending on Simon's provisions of food and wine.

While Tabitha wanted to celebrate the marriage of his youngest daughter, her eyes were focused on the back door. She prayed that Elohim, in His almighty power, would block the entry if He must. Keep her son working with the ship merchant named Agathon this afternoon instead of ruining Bethany's celebration.

This day was for Bethany and her bridegroom. For Simon the Tanner to welcome Joshua, a Hebrew fisherman, into their household.

Bethany and Joshua sat under the covered peristyle at a table spread with exotic fruits and flatbread and bowls of oil spiced with herbs, listening to the musicians play the harp and flute. The song they played was one from the Psalms, about God's redemption from their enemy.

While Tabitha hadn't had a formal wedding of her own, these celebrations reminded her of the man she'd been blessed to marry twenty-five years ago. The man she still missed after his boat was splintered in a storm. The moment that she'd met Isaac, she'd wanted to marry him, even though he had little money to support them and she certainly had no dowry to offer. Only herself.

Eighteen years ago, she'd offered herself again, this time as a mother to a baby she'd loved with all her heart. But lately neither her love nor the love of their Father had been enough.

She'd asked Matthias to stay away from the wedding feast. Not because she didn't love him—there was no one on this earth she loved more—but because her son had changed in the past year. He'd become enamored with Bethany, the talented musician who led their church in worship. A quiet woman who was gifted with song.

But when Matthias asked for Simon's permission to marry his daughter, the man had rejected his proposal.

Nothing made Tabitha's son angrier than rejection. After Simon turned Matthias away, it was as if Matthias crawled back into himself for a season, became the child who'd screamed for life on Joppa's rubbish pile.

Within a week of Matthias declaring his intentions, Simon announced the betrothal between his daughter and Joshua, a devout follower of the Messiah. And Matthias had been irate at what he considered to be a personal affront, a humiliating slap across the face—humiliation that motivated him to right what he thought had gone horribly wrong.

Irrationally, Matthias was convinced that he could win both Bethany and Simon over. He continued to engage Bethany at their services in what was clearly painful for her and Joshua and all of the disciples in their community. Matthias was relentless, but only the bridegroom could issue a divorce for his betrothed wife. Joshua intended to keep his promise, and Simon was equally as determined to have Joshua for a son.

Tabitha took a sip of the honeyed wine as she watched Zoe, her fellow seamstress and friend, tap on a battery of stone jars with her six-year-old son, pretending the jars were drums. Like Tabitha and Matthias used to do when he was young.

The two of them had been close in those early years. Then when he completed school, he followed through on his plans to oversee the distribution of clothing that his mother and her friends sewed. He rented the market stall, and for months now he had excelled at selling their tunics.

When her son wanted something, he didn't let anyone stop him.

Simon stepped up beside her, his gaze on the back door. "Where's Matthias?"

He'd enlisted his brother to watch the entry, and while he didn't say it was to keep Matthias out, she knew the reason. The entire wedding party knew that Matthias was not welcome here.

She took another sip. "He is helping Agathon load the *Chiron*." The ship that would begin its voyage across the Mediterranean Sea in the morning.

"He's leaving?"

Tabitha respected this man, the leader of their community, but his tone devastated her heart. No mother wanted to hear another wish her child, no matter what age, to be gone.

"He will stay in Joppa," she said. "He is selling our garments in the market."

Simon looked doubtful. "Perhaps it's time for you to let him go, Tabitha."

"I will let him go when God requires it of me."

"We always pray for him," Simon said. "And will welcome him back to the community when he's ready."

Tabitha simply nodded as Simon returned to his role as host, mingling among the fifty or so guests who'd come to celebrate this occasion. They would welcome Matthias back when he was ready to leave Simon's daughter alone.

Someone shouted behind her, and the wine burned in her stomach. She didn't want to look, knowing she'd be forever scarred, but she forced herself to turn.

Simon's brother tried to stop him, but all it took was one punch and Matthias landed him on the floor. Then this son she loved more than anything stormed across the courtyard, guests parting around him like dazed fish in the Red Sea.

She lifted her skirt and ran toward the banquet table, but it was too late. Matthias swept his arm across their feast, spilling the fruits and meat and expensive oils across the dirt floor, splashing the fine garments of the wedding party.

"Stop!" she shouted, but he didn't listen.

His arm covered with food, his face drenched in a drunken sweat, Matthias lunged for the bride as if she were a bag of flax that he'd purchased in the market. As if he could carry her away.

As if Bethany would go willingly.

Tabitha froze. When had this boy she loved turned into a monster?

Bethany screamed when Matthias tried to kiss her, her wedding veil falling onto the ruined table as she struggled to get away. Her distress seemed to rouse Matthias for the slightest of moments, until Joshua tried to rescue her.

Matthias's intoxicated state allowed no room for failure. As Joshua tugged on Bethany's waist, Matthias yanked on her hair. And an entire clump of those beautiful honey-brown locks came out in his hand.

The hair finally wakened him from his trance, to all the people staring, to Bethany's tears, to the hair he'd dropped on the ground. Then Simon, the leader of their small church, the father of the bride, pummeled her son.

Zoe was at Tabitha's side, arms wrapped around her in love as Matthias struggled against the men who lifted him, as he fought against their grip as they carried him away. Tabitha had begged God to keep her son away from this wedding. Why hadn't He answered her prayer?

Several of the guests turned toward her as if an epilogue might close this tragedy, her the remaining actor to narrate it onstage.

"I must go," Tabitha said.

Zoe kissed her cheek and then escorted her to the front entry, insisting that Simon's brother unbar the door.

She found Matthias in a heap on the cobblestone, like one of the flighty hyrax that lived in the desert, bolting out of the rocks to defend his territory and then scrambling back inside.

But it was too late for him to hide now.

"Get up!" she demanded. When he didn't move, she reached for his ear and pulled him to his feet as if he were three. "Why would you do this to me?"

To *her*, that's what she'd meant to say. Why had he done this to Bethany and to himself?

"It's not about you, *Imma*."

"It's about all of us. Our community."

He shoved her away. "I'm no longer part of that community."

"We'll talk in the morning," she said. Once the wine had dissolved, when he realized what he'd done.

His words slurred when he spoke again, his cheek swollen from Simon's fist. "Talking won't solve this."

"Go home, Matthias."

He leaned against the stones of Simon's house, his legs wobbly. And she remembered again those first years with him, his long struggle to walk. "Do you want me to take you home?"

"I don't want anything," he said. "Not from you."

She left him there then and stayed at the feast for another hour, trying to repair some of the damage by cleaning the floor. All was silent when she returned home to the villa, and she was grateful for the mercy of rest.

In the morning, Matthias would awaken with some sort of peace in his mind.

In the morning, they'd make amends.

# CHAPTER TWO

*A Year Later*

Twelve denarii for this lovely cloak," Tabitha called to a shopper as he passed her merchant stall.

Boldness was a virtue in Joppa's crowded marketplace, but her friend had no appreciation for bartering. Instead of selling her garments, Zoe had ducked behind the stall's wooden slats as if she had an urgent mandate to retie the leather strap on her sandal.

"Eleven denarii," Tabitha bargained. The man ignored her offer, but villagers who visited this weekly bazaar were here to shop, and Zoe made some of the finest tunics in all of Judea. The apathy of one person wouldn't deter them. As an almost thirty-year-old widow, Zoe needed the income to cover her expenses and provide for her son.

Turning, Tabitha held the linen garment up a little higher, calling out to another shopper. If they didn't offer an initial price, Zoe would never sell one of the linen garments she'd so meticulously stitched. Both the robes and the outer traveling cloaks would be left hanging on these hooks instead of being replaced with new merchandise next week.

"Please." Tabitha knelt beside her friend. "You have to at least try."

"I'll make another garment, even better than these," Zoe said. "No one will be able to pass it by."

"But you must sell something today, for David's sake."

Strands from Zoe's coiled brown hair fell loose when she shook her head. "I can't bargain nearly as well as you."

"You don't need to barter. Just offer a fair price."

"I'll pay eight denarii for your cloak," a man above the counter said.

Zoe opened her mouth to respond, but Tabitha stopped her. She recognized the man's voice and knew he was quite pleased with his insult, but she refused to let him torment her or Zoe on this fine spring morning.

"Fifteen denarii for you, Agathon." She stood slowly, brushing the dust off her maroon-colored robe. "A bargain."

With a sweep of his arm, the tassels dangling from Agathon's sleeve brushed across her counter, the smell of soured milk tainting her stall. "You taunt me, Dorcas."

*Gazelle,* that's what her name meant. A beautiful creature in the wilderness. The man always used the Greek translation although she preferred the Aramaic version—Tabitha—and he knew it.

Tabitha. Dorcas. Imma. All names that she answered to, although no one had called her Imma—Mother—in almost a year.

"You taunt me," she retorted. "Eight denarii won't even pay for the material."

"You should select less expensive material if you want to charge a fortune," he said, the copper amulet around his neck swaying with each word. "Not even Zeus in all his wealth could afford the clothing that you and Zoe are trying to sell."

"And yet you come to our stall...."

He glanced to his right, to the busy alleyway filled with merchants and their wares, at the smoke billowing from the fires of entrepreneurs who roasted and sold chestnuts and meat to those passing through Joppa for the day.

"Out of desperation," he said.

She held out another cloak, the sky-blue color and simple lines on it much too plain for a man who took pride in his self-indulgence. And much too small for the vessel built from his extravagant meals. "Your Selene would have loved the simplicity of this one."

It was too late for him to buy his wife a gift, but Selene would have worn this with grace. Unlike her husband, Selene had been a kind soul and a bold one who had chosen to follow the Way even when her husband mocked her for it.

While Tabitha despised Agathon the merchant—her husband's business partner—she had adored his wife.

The man shook his head. "I'm not here to buy a cloak."

She drew the material back against her. "Why exactly are you here?"

"I could ask you the same question. You don't have to work like a common—"

She stopped him. "I'm helping Zoe sell the beautiful garments she's made."

"I would like Zoe to make something for me." He scanned the small space behind Tabitha. "Where is she?"

With her eyes still on Agathon, Tabitha leaned over between the hanging garments and tugged on Zoe's arm. Even though she lacked business sense, her friend had grown legions in her skills as a seamstress. A commission from this man would bolster her reputation and ultimately her sales with men and women alike.

Zoe rose slowly, as if she were a goddess emerging from her palace. "Hello, Agathon."

He glared at her. "Were you napping?"

"She was resting," Tabitha explained. "Our business has been quite brisk this morning."

Agathon waved his hand, brushing against the bulky set of keys that jangled from the cord around his waist. From behind the haze of smoke emerged Korinna, the beautiful young woman who had been Selene's maidservant until she died. It seemed that she'd been hiding like Zoe.

The woman moved slowly toward them, her head down, her once white garment now stained and worn. Selene would have insisted that Korinna wear something more fitting, especially since she was now a woman of at least fifteen.

When the young woman looked up, Tabitha saw sadness in her green eyes. And a glint of fear. Tabitha understood well that fear. She had been terrified when she was fifteen.

Korinna must miss her former mistress, even more than Tabitha did. While Agathon, to Tabitha's knowledge, wasn't cruel, he was a harsh master who demanded much from his employees and slaves. And from a lovely woman like this—

Tabitha shuddered to think what he might expect now that Selene was gone.

Tabitha nudged Zoe's hand under the counter, prompting her to speak. "Would you like us to make a tunic?"

"I can't hear you!" he barked.

"A new tunic," Zoe said, louder now in the face of this lion. "Would you like me to make a day tunic for her?"

"No." Agathon shoved the younger woman forward. "I need you to make her a wedding garment."

The cobblestones seemed to drop out from under Tabitha, plunging her into the sea. She didn't really want to know the answer to the question she must ask. "Whom will she be marrying?"

"Me, of course."

Four months, that was how long Selene had been gone. Many men married soon after becoming widowers, to one of their slaves even, but Agathon was at least three decades older than this woman who was still very much a girl. While no one else might balk at this arrangement, Tabitha was devastated for both Korinna and the memory of her dear friend.

"Not too expensive," Agathon insisted. "I'm not made of gold."

He was a savvy businessman and merchant, the owner of the *Chiron*—one of the ships Isaac had built—that traveled from Joppa to ports across the Mediterranean, distributing cargo between Greece and Egypt and Jerusalem. The ship that had stolen Matthias away.

Agathon knew that no one in this city, perhaps not even in the whole region of Judea, would sell him a bridal garment for less than twenty denarii.

Tabitha set the blue tunic on the counter and crossed her arms. "Exactly how much would you like to pay for this garment?"

"Fifteen denarii, the same as that cloak."

She glanced over at Zoe's blanched face. The material for a wedding garment would cost almost fifteen denarii. "I suppose I can—"

"Eighteen denarii," Tabitha blurted, "with one exception."

He crossed his arms over his imposing frame. "I'm not here to bargain."

"Then you've come to the wrong stall."

Tabitha dropped her hands to the counter. "This exception, Agathon, or the garment costs twenty denarii. A price we all know you can well afford."

He eyed her. "Perhaps she doesn't need a new tunic to marry after all. Not all women do."

She stiffened at the words, his knowledge the pinnacle of bargaining power. Isaac hadn't meant to wound her when he told Agathon that they couldn't afford a wedding tunic for Tabitha when they'd married, but still the reminder cut into her heart, provoking a flame.

Her seven years with Isaac had only been a glimpse in this life, but what beautiful years they had been, even when their income was meager.

Korinna would never know love like that, not with a man like Agathon. He only wanted what his first wife hadn't been able to give him, what Tabitha hadn't been able to give Isaac—a legacy of a son to take over his business.

Perhaps that's why she and Selene had become close friends. While Tabitha had been honored to raise Matthias as her own, she'd lost her husband before she'd given him the gift of a child. And Selene had lost two children soon after they were born. The two women had bonded over what they'd lost and then found in their Messiah, their kindred hearts blossoming into a friendship.

"Every bride needs a wedding garment, no matter whom she must marry."

His eyes narrowed. "What is your exception?"

"The wedding tunic is the most prized piece of a woman's wardrobe." Tabitha ran her hands across the blue material. "No garment is more special than the one she stitches for her wedding day."

His thick fingers drummed on the counter. "I am not a man of sentiment."

"I never suspected you were." She leaned toward him. "But I am confident that you are a man of sound business principle."

"You are proposing that I purchase the materials from your storehouse and then Korinna sews the garment herself?"

She didn't dare glance at Zoe. "That is my proposal. Eighteen denarii for the finest linen along with thread for her to embroider the collar and sleeves."

He turned toward Korinna. "Do you know how to sew?"

"No—"

He shook his head, clearly disgusted by her lack. "Then we have no bargain here."

Tabitha's mind tumbled like a wave as she studied Korinna. The silent cry from the woman's gaze reminded her of that fateful night in the dump long ago when her son had cried out for help.

Her gaze dropped to Korinna's capable hands, and a new thought emerged, one that would honor her deceased friend and perhaps help this young woman. "I will buy her from you, Agathon. At a price even you agree is fair. She can apprentice with me—"

"She's not for sale."

Tabitha brushed her hands over the linen cloak hanging next to her, allowing time for Agathon to consider a compromise. "Then I will teach her how to sew."

He studied her face as if he might find a secret motive hidden in the lines that had begun to fold themselves across her face. "Why would you do such a thing?"

"Because every woman needs a wedding garment, and you've stated clearly that you cannot afford one for your future wife."

He snorted. "Your insults, subtle or not, have no effect on me."

"Insults?" she asked innocently. "I have no interest except for your good."

"And how can her learning to sew be for my good?"

Tabitha smiled. "Because Korinna can use this new skill to increase the income of your household. Eighteen denarii for her to make a garment worth at least twenty-five. A tunic that will impress your neighbors and an education that will return tenfold in time."

He contemplated her offer.

"And Korinna can sew clothes for your other slaves, like Selene used to do. The money you would save…"

"I'm leaving for Athens within a week," he said. "And I'll be gone for at least two months."

Her heart caught in her chest, its beat of life seeming to fade away. "The *Chiron* will be here soon?"

"Any day."

Tabitha glanced down at the sea as if the ship might emerge from one of the thousand crystals that lit its watery cloak.

He leaned closer. "When I return, I expect a tunic for the wedding and a garment for each of the five servants in my home."

"I will instruct Korinna on how to make the tunic for eighteen denarii, and then she and Zoe will sew robes for your staff at six denarii each." He stepped back with a brisk nod, ready to continue his shopping in other stalls, but Tabitha stopped him. "If it's agreeable to Korinna, of course."

"If what's agreeable?"

Korinna's eyes widened with surprise when Tabitha turned toward her. "Would you like to learn how to sew?"

The younger woman didn't speak, didn't even nod, but Tabitha saw the flash of agreement in her green eyes, only a glimpse before she looked away.

"It doesn't matter if she's agreeable or not—"

"Of course it does." Tabitha smiled. She'd caught this fish of a man, snaring him firmly on the hook of his pride.

He reached for Korinna's wrist. "She will do what I say."

Tabitha wasn't quite ready for him to leave. "Twenty-four denarii now for all the garments." She put out her hand. "You can pay the remaining twenty-four when we are finished."

He retrieved the money from his girdle and tossed the silver coins across the counter. Before he reached for Korinna's arm, Tabitha saw a hint of a smile on the girl's face.

A skill like sewing, Tabitha had learned, could open up an entirely new world to any woman, free or enslaved. This gift would be for both Korinna and Selene.

Tabitha shook her head. "That poor woman…"

"His day tunic was worth about eighteen denarii." Zoe leaned back against the stall, sweat beaded across her forehead. "How will she survive being married to him?"

"I suppose he was a decent husband to Selene."

"That's because he loved her." Zoe hung the cloak on a hook beside their other wares. "He doesn't love Korinna nor will he ever, no matter how beautiful she is."

She couldn't rescue everyone—she'd learned that long ago—but Tabitha wished that she could rescue Korinna from a fate some would consider worse than death.

If God redeemed Agathon, no matter how much she despised the man, perhaps Korinna could be redeemed as well. "I will invite Agathon again to church, so he can hear the teachings from Peter."

Zoe sighed. "You are a better woman than I."

"Not better, but if faith in Jesus saved him, think of what would happen to her—"

"His own pride would have to be crucified before he would follow the teachings of a Jewish carpenter."

Tabitha's gaze wandered back to the blaze of blue sea, longing for the *Chiron* to journey home soon. "If Jesus beat death, anything is possible."

"You're thinking of Matthias, aren't you?" Zoe asked.

Tabitha wiped her hand across her cheeks. "Always."

Zoe reached for her hand and squeezed it. "If Jesus can conquer death—"

"Anything is possible," Tabitha repeated, dumping one of the denarii into Zoe's hand. The rest she would use to buy the material.

A miracle was what she—what they both—needed.

Only a miracle would bring her son home.

# CHAPTER THREE

Tabitha scooted off her wool-filled mattress in the lantern of moonlight and watched light glitter across the Mediterranean Sea. From the upper chamber of her home, under the temporary arbor made of brushwood and leaves, she could see both the water and slope of Joppa's hill with its dozens of villas clustered together, all of them clutching the rocky cliff.

Sometimes she climbed the steps to this chamber during the day, searching the sea for the return of the *Chiron*, but she couldn't see the ships that arrived during the night. The crewmen anchored far from the precarious shoreline, waiting until dawn to unload their goods.

This waiting on her son, for almost a year now, was anguish. In these dark hours when she was alone, when sleep was as elusive as a mustard seed in the sand, she wished she could press through the waiting, dig deeper to find answers—healing—for herself and this headstrong man she loved. And beg his forgiveness for exploding in anger.

But God had called her to wait.

With the stick and mud walls behind her, Tabitha leaned against the parapet and searched for a flicker of candlelight or oil lantern hanging from its bow. The moon had begun its descent toward the chasm where seawater enveloped the night, where the ocean buried this orb of cool light. Morning, she prayed, would reveal a ship. She'd be the first one waiting at the harbor, long before the sun rose. Praying that her son had finally returned home.

She returned to the mattress and closed her eyes. Goats bleated below her villa and a cow bellowed in the distance, the animals basking in their reprieve from the sun. Her Greek neighbors would petition Hypnos to lure them back to sleep in his quiet underworld. But she'd forsaken this god along with the many other Greek gods who vied for power in this area overseen by a Hebrew government but occupied by a combination of Greeks, Hellenistic Jews who'd embraced Greek culture, and Hebrew Jews who remained devoted to the law.

She belonged to a fourth group that held no political power in Joppa, but she prayed this group would grow in influence as Greek and Hebrew alike chose to follow in the steps of Jesus, a man who'd changed everything for her.

Others might see a widow like she was as worthless as the rubbish pile above Joppa, but not the Messiah. While Jesus was on this earth, He'd elevated women who'd been grieving, given them a calling far beyond their mantle of grief. He had respected widows and so did His followers. They'd welcomed her after Isaac's death and the orphan boy who became her son.

The hostilities toward the followers of the Way had been growing. Ever since the disciples of Christ were banned from entering the synagogue, their community had been meeting in the courtyard of her villa for worship and prayer. They'd gather later today, away from the criticism of men like Agathon.

In a few hours the sun would reappear like an ember in the east, but she didn't have the patience to wait for its flame. She scooted off the mattress again, then slipped on her sandals and smoothed out the wrinkles on her tunic before rinsing her face in the basin. Not that anyone cared about the face or hair of a forty-three-year-old widow, but while she was a firm believer in modesty, she also believed every woman, married or not, should tend the beauty entrusted to her.

After arranging a veil over her tousled hair, the brown strands threaded with gray, Tabitha shuffled down the exterior steps into the vestibule. Her son wouldn't care how she looked, but she hoped—prayed—that he still cared about her.

Matthias had been searching for years for the man he wanted to become, and after Bethany's wedding, he'd run away from her and their entire community, trying to find himself on sea or on land, in Israel or Greece. Some thought the moon and its stars controlled their lives, convinced that the stars took pleasure in tormenting the humans below, but every night she prayed that whenever Matthias saw the moonlight, the breadth of stars, he would remember the God who had sent His Son into their world to set him free from the powers that sought to imprison him. That, as he searched for the goodness of God, he would find himself in the midst of it all.

She stole quietly through the vestibule, taking care not to awaken Niles and Glykera, a husband and wife who'd been part of her household since she'd first arrived in Joppa. They would know she had gone to the harbor to see if Matthias had finally come home.

Tabitha slipped outside, to the narrow street dividing the homes and shops and inns that housed boatmen and travelers alike, and hurried down to the harbor. She found a flat rock to sit on near the harbor's breakwater, a rock barrier created to keep waves from slamming into the lower part of their city. Mist had settled over the sea like a curtain, and she prayed its lifting would reveal sails of the wooden ship that Isaac and his men had built long ago.

Many years ago a prophet named Jonah had sailed from this port, heading the opposite direction from the city where God had called him to go, but he couldn't outrun a holy God. Instead of letting him continue, God brought Jonah to a place of desperation until he submitted to the will of the One who wanted to rescue an entire city from its sins. A God who didn't—*couldn't* in His holiness—tolerate evil. A God, she believed, who desired goodness and redemption for all men and women. Hebrew, Roman, or Greek.

In lieu of sending more prophets, Elohim finally sent His Son to this land. Belief in Jesus—in His conquering of death— could save Matthias. That's what the apostle Peter had taught through his letters to their community, and she believed it. Jesus had saved Isaac and then, even when she'd failed misera- bly, saved her. Jesus could also rescue her son.

Her heart pumped faster in the stillness as she wondered what would happen if Matthias really did come home. What would she say to him? And would he forgive her for failing him?

She had not been the mother that Matthias had needed, especially in his early years when she felt as if she were drowning in her own sorrow after losing Isaac, forgetting Matthias had lost much as well. Even if he couldn't remember those hours before he'd been abandoned or the men who'd tried to enslave him, she should have understood his sorrow from this loss, empathized with his fears as a child.

After removing her sandals, Tabitha dipped her chafed toes into the sea. The salt stung them, but the water also carried healing in its sting. Like forgiveness to a heartache. Love to envelop a wound. Needle and thread to fix what was once torn.

Light sparked in the east, trickling across her feet, and she gazed into the distance again, searching for what she still couldn't see.

"I thought I'd find you here."

As Zoe crept over the rocks, her long hair flowing across the front of her robe, Tabitha scanned the mishmash of hillside villas until she found the small house where Zoe and her son rented a room.

"Where is David?" she asked as Zoe lowered herself onto another rock.

"He was fast asleep when I left."

"But he'll worry about you," Tabitha said, the familiar panic swelling in her chest.

"I already told him that I'd be gone this morning."

Tabitha wanted to tell her to return home and cling to this boy for as long as he was willing to stay, but Zoe was a good mother. Faithful. David wouldn't run away to Greece.

Zoe nodded toward the sea. "What will you say to him when he comes back?"

"That I'm glad he's home," Tabitha replied, tears flooding her eyes. The ship had returned four times since Matthias had left Joppa, and each time she'd been told that he had stayed in Athens. Her heart, she feared, would break if he wasn't on board this morning.

Zoe held out her hand, an invitation to remind Tabitha that she wasn't alone. "Is that all?"

"And I'll tell him I'm sorry."

"You've been a good mother to him," Zoe said.

But she hadn't been good. In her anger, she'd pushed her already troubled son away.

Tabitha grasped her friend's hand, the tears now flowing down her cheeks.

"May I pray?" Zoe asked.

When Tabitha nodded, her friend prayed as the tide brushed over their feet, asking God to bring Matthias home. Asking God to redeem his life.

Others began gathering around the harbor, waiting for the mist to clear away. And, like her, waiting for someone they loved—a son or husband or father—to come home.

If not today, perhaps the ship would arrive tomorrow. They'd all gather along this shore until the *Chiron* finally made its way back to Joppa.

Sunlight crept past the crowd, to the edge of the gray veil that hid the sea. Moments later, a rowboat broke through the fog and a cheer rose up among the crowd. While those waiting still couldn't see the ship, the oarsmen had managed to find shore.

With Zoe's hand in hers, Tabitha scanned the heads of the four rowers. She didn't recognize any of them with their long bangs and beards, so different from Matthias's neatly trimmed hair before he left home.

Her son wasn't among the first sailors to arrive.

As the mist cleared, she could see the square sail of the *Chiron* stamped against the sky. Perhaps Matthias was still on board.

"Breathe," Zoe whispered.

She inhaled the salty air as a lighter was pushed from Joppa's quay to fetch passengers and crewmen and perhaps some of the cargo marked for Jerusalem. Most of these items would be delivered eventually via camel and donkey to the city market, where they'd bring Agathon enough denarii to buy a hundred wedding dresses for his bride.

Minutes passed and then a good hour as others drifted away. And she and Zoe waited together.

Tabitha couldn't seem to move. "The women will be arriving soon."

The small group who gathered three mornings each week at her home, sewing together before their church—*Ekklesia*—met for the midday meal and worship.

Zoe released her hand. "I will go."

"Fetch David first."

"Of course," Zoe said. It was understood—she always brought David with her when they sewed—but Tabitha still needed to say it.

"Tell the women—"

"I will tell them you were delayed. They need know nothing more."

"Thank you."

Zoe kissed both her cheeks. "God will provide."

Tabitha nodded. "He already has."

"Provide for your heart," her friend added. "For it to be whole."

# CHAPTER FOUR

Wind swept across the *Chiron*, but the deck's cedar planks didn't shudder from the wind or waves. Instead the ship gently rocked as one body, heel to toe and back again. A constant sway of movement that Matthias had embraced in this past year.

His feet weren't used to solid ground. In fact, he wasn't even certain anymore what was solid—or true. His father had built this ship—at least, the man who might have been his father if an accident hadn't stolen his life away. The old captain spoke of Isaac the Shipbuilder often, of his fine carpentry skills and knowledge of the sea. Isaac had somehow found balance between respect and adventure as he'd learned how to traverse the unpredictable sea until the gods of this sea decided to fight back.

Matthias dropped a coil of rope near the stern, beside a wood carving of the civilized centaur called Chiron. On land, the city of Joppa clung to the hillside like barnacles on the hull of this ship, only a reef separating him and his home.

*Home.*

He didn't want to be here…or there, on the hill. Unlike the other sailors, eager to step onto shore, he would wait on the ship until it was time to sail back to Greece.

Athens had been as foreign to him as his father, but full of life and a culture that distracted him from the memories of the woman he'd intended to marry in Joppa. The residents of Athens promoted all things spiritual with their worship of idols on the Acropolis, yet in spite of their obsession with spirituality, the city was devoid of faith. At least, any real faith. The gods were much lauded, but as far as he could tell, impotent in power.

Those he'd met in Athens had asked what he believed, and he'd stumbled over words to respond. In Greece, a man was welcome to believe in any of the gods he wanted, except in one true God. No one wanted to answer to a single god. They expected the gods to answer them.

He didn't know what he believed, but what he wanted to know, what he'd yet been unable to find, was if the supposed God above gods—Elohim—was real or if this god of his mother's was as fake as Artemis, Demeter, and Zeus.

Real was what he needed. To be able to touch God. Understand and experience Him. Not offer sacrifices to wood or stone or give his allegiance to an invisible god who seemed as impotent as those on Athens's esteemed hill.

He'd been berated in Athens for asking so many questions, but he couldn't understand what was wrong with asking. Without questioning, he would never understand why a god who was supposed to love seemed so distant. Why this god who had seemingly rescued him from a rubbish pile had given the woman he loved to another and left him without a future. Nineteen full years on this earth and he still hadn't found firm footing on land.

Perhaps he could still find the truth in Athens or one of the islands where this ship ported. He certainly hadn't found God in Joppa.

He glanced down at his left hand, at the stump in place of a thumb. His mark for life. Every time it slipped out from under his tunic, he was reminded that his own parents hadn't wanted him.

After the wedding feast, he'd run as far as he could from Joppa. He wanted to experience life away from this place, and he'd embraced these months to the fullest, meeting plenty of people—plenty of women—in Athens. Women who had been quite accommodating to a man anxious to experience the world.

But nothing satisfied him—not the travel or gods or women. Nothing on this ship—or across the sea—had steadied the rocking of his soul.

He nudged a burlap sack with his toe. The cargo of pottery, metals, fabric, and a variety of fruits had been unloaded from the ship, carried to shore by lighters. The other boatmen had probably forgotten him by now as they enjoyed an afternoon of revelry. Although Joppa didn't compare to Athens in its offerings, they would find plenty of amusement before they returned to sea. His mother would never even have to know that he'd been just fathoms from home.

If she knew…she'd wait by the quay all afternoon, waiting to tell him how much she and God loved him. And while he didn't regret much in his leaving Joppa, he wished he'd said goodbye to her. Arriving home and then leaving again…he would break her heart even more than he'd already done. She didn't deserve this pain.

He didn't want to hurt her, but he'd changed in the past year and she wouldn't be pleased. Still she would care for him, just like she cared for everyone around her, cared in such a way that others flocked to her as she opened up her arms, her home, to all in need. He was one of many she'd brought into her fold.

But he was no longer a baby in need of a savior. He was old enough now and perfectly capable to save himself.

"Go home, Matthias," a man behind him said.

It was the Egyptian sailor they called Amon, his dark chest bare in the heat of the day as if he really were the god of sun.

"In time," Matthias said, his gaze returning to the cluster of homes beyond the reef.

"You'll have to go eventually."

"I never have to return—"

Amon draped his arms over the side. "You must have a woman waiting for you here."

One who loved him dearly…and one who'd already married another.

"Only my mother," he said.

"The most faithful of women," Amon said. "You are a blessed man."

"She loves me, perhaps too much."

Wind drove a wave into the side of their boat, and the men swayed with its swell. "Is it possible to love one too much?"

Matthias sighed. "It's possible."

"Ah, you feel as if it's knocked you over."

"I feel—" he started, but he didn't know exactly how he felt.

A speck—the flat lighter boat—moved toward them, his last opportunity to join the others on shore before the boatmen began loading new cargo for their return voyage west.

Amon nodded at the approaching boat. "It's coming to fetch us both."

"I'll stay on board with the captain," Matthias said. "Make sure there's no trouble here."

"You never stay on the ship...."

"I've never had reason to."

Amon wouldn't understand how hard it was to go home, then leave once again with the tension separating him and his mother. He had no desire to wound her again, and her heart would be placated in the busyness of her good work if he simply let her be.

He couldn't see his mother nor could he bear to see the woman he'd once loved—still loved—with his entire being. In the past year, he'd done everything he could to erase her image from his mind so he only saw her now in his dreams.

Instead of going to Joppa, he could stay on the safety of this vessel that could weather any storm, then return to Greece. Perhaps, one day, that great country would become home.

"You spoke once about a Bethany," Amon said.

The very name shot like a bolt through Matthias, a spark to reignite a flame, and he needed to douse it before it raged through him once again. "I must have been drunk."

"Very," Amon replied. "You said something about killing her husband."

"I didn't kill him," he said although he'd thought plenty about it.

Amon eyed the lighter again before looking back at him. "Perhaps you could still marry, once she divorces the man who stole her from you."

"Her family would never condone a divorce."

"Then take her back to Athens with us. She wouldn't need to obtain a divorce to live with you there."

Matthias looked back at the villas in Joppa. He couldn't see the lines of Bethany's home, but he knew exactly where it was located. Was she still living there—she and her rotten husband? Would she divorce him? No, Matthias didn't think Bethany would break her vow.

Perhaps, after this year, her heart still longed for him as he did for her. If she went to Athens with him, perhaps Joshua would be the one to divorce her.

If Bethany still loved him, perhaps she would go.

Amon dropped the rope ladder over the side of the ship. "Why didn't you stay in Athens?"

"I needed the money...."

"Because you spend instead of save."

"I spend what I need and work when I must."

Amon climbed over the port side, his feet settling into the rungs so he could lower himself to the waiting boat.

"You'll regret it if you don't visit your mother," Amon said. "And perhaps this Bethany as well."

But the truth was, he already had a lifetime of regrets. One more wouldn't make a bit of difference now.

# CHAPTER FIVE

Tabitha paced across the damp stones until the lighter arrived for the last time into the quay. An African sailor stepped onto the rocky shore, a man who'd shaken his head sadly when she inquired about her son.

Matthias, it seemed, still hadn't come home.

Was he in Athens? She'd asked the boatman in both Hebrew and Greek, but he had no response. Either he didn't speak either language or he didn't know where Matthias had gone.

If only she had news, to know that he was safe. Tomorrow she'd inquire at the inns, after the wine had settled in the bellies of the arriving boatmen, after she'd rested her heart. Perhaps another man would know what happened to Matthias.

The wondering had haunted her heart day and night for the past year. She knew where her husband was, his body interred in the tomb above Joppa, his soul secure in the heavens, but where was her son? If Isaac were still alive, he would take the *Chiron* back to Athens, stopping at every port along the way if he must, to search.

Of course, if Isaac were still here, she wouldn't have visited the dump on that day Matthias had needed her, so they would have no son. He would have died, she'd no doubt, in the hands of those traders.

What if Matthias needed her now, wherever he was? He might be ill or wounded or enslaved on an island between here and Greece, and she could do nothing to help him.

If he was well, would he ever return to her?

The scriptures were clear that a man should leave his father and mother, cleave to his wife, but Matthias had no wife. Or had he married in Athens? If he had married, she'd probably never see him again.

Her stomach rolled as she walked the cobblestone path back up to her villa, nodding to friends she passed. Her tears were gone but she didn't stop to speak with anyone, afraid the tears would flow rapidly again if someone inquired about him.

Perhaps Agathon—if she paid the man—would search for Matthias in Athens. She'd clothe Korinna for the rest of her life if Agathon found him.

The doorway to her villa was open for the many guests who would come and go freely today. Isaac had overseen the building of this home with its two stories of stone, a lofty courtyard, and an open chamber above to bask in the cool night air. They'd both hoped for frequent visitors and a host of children to fill it.

The second story played host to those rooms where they slept each winter, but instead of harboring a large family, several of the rooms stored the material that she acquired through traveling merchants, material she transformed into clothing for women and children who couldn't afford it on their own. A new tunic or shawl or cloak was her way of offering renewed life to someone who needed it. A glimmer of hope in the mist.

When Isaac died, he'd left her with this beautiful villa and enough income—if she used it wisely—to sustain her until God called her home. And the Lord had provided more than enough denarii to pay for the cloth and thread for the widows who wanted to learn how to sew. Widows who would be impoverished without work.

So the women all worked together to create garments worn by the wealthy here and in Jerusalem, taking turns in the market stall for those who were in earnest need of money. The women simply reimbursed her for the supplies when they sold their wares, and she reinvested the money into someone else. And Agathon, much to his chagrin, still paid her a percentage of every shipment that he brought through Joppa's port, fulfilling an old agreement with Isaac that a magistrate insisted he continue as long as he sailed the *Chiron*.

Taking a deep breath, Tabitha prayed for strength as she walked between the worn frescoes of ships on plastered vestibule walls, toward a courtyard where she grew figs and prized lemons along with herbs and the flowers she took each week to Isaac's grave.

Her widowed friends would be waiting—eight of these sisters who gathered here to sew. *Rhapsodies*, they called themselves, from the Greek words for sewing and song. Like a rhapsode who traveled from village to village reciting poetry, these women were doing more than sewing garments. They were stitching together a song with their lives, a way to worship God and provide for themselves and their families.

Others might think them hopeless, but the Messiah had offered them a freedom—a hope—they'd never dreamed about. None of them, including her, were any longer slaves to their situation or to the laws that proved impossible to keep.

The needs of these women were great. They relied on her to be strong, but in their kindness they blessed her, especially on days like this when she didn't feel strong at all.

"Tabitha!" Miriam—one of her sisters—greeted her, kissing her cheek. "We were worried."

She glanced across the stone birdbath, the centerpiece of this courtyard, to Zoe sitting on the pillows of a marble bench beside an older member, helping her sew a seam in the fabric draped across her lap. A gentle smile crossed Zoe's lips before she returned to her work.

Smoke hovered above the clay oven at the far end of the courtyard, near the entrance to the kitchen. A channel of fresh water ran across the width of this outdoor space whenever it was released from the tanks above Joppa, water they used in the kitchen and to water her plants.

Clematis blossoms draped over the shaded peristyle that circled her courtyard. Near the stream, under the shade of a lemon tree, David played quietly with a handful of smooth stones while two chickens pecked a pile of grain beside him. Before Matthias left, David had often followed him around like a chick trailing its mother.

"I had personal business to attend to," Tabitha explained before picking up the woven basket that contained her needles and thread and the lime-colored linen purchased from Galilee.

She never had personal business on Monday, Wednesday, or Friday mornings—and her sisters knew it—but the hope for Matthias and his return was one that she held close to her heart.

The women returned to their chatting, counseling each other on their work and helping when necessary. Most of them knew how to sew on their own now, and they created beautiful garments, some of them more detailed with their embroidery than any piece Tabitha had ever made. The truth was, Tabitha needed them in her life just as much, maybe even more, than they needed her.

Her basket in hand, Tabitha moved toward one of six divans arranged under the peristyle. Instead of selling her work, Tabitha prayed over each piece as she stitched, asking God to guide her to a woman or child who needed it. This tunic would be for a child. A boy, perhaps.

As she began to sew, someone knocked on the open front door and the clapping sound of brass echoed through the courtyard. Tabitha caught her breath. No one who visited on these mornings ever knocked, and no one with the Joppa church knocked either when they attended the noon worship and meal. Her door was always open during the week, ready to welcome any guest who wanted to come inside.

Was it possible that she'd missed Matthias among the crowd at the harbor? Had he decided to come home after all?

But why would her son knock to enter his own home when the door was wide open?

She poked her finger with the needle and quickly lowered it, waiting like the rest of them for Glykera, her maidservant, to escort their visitor inside.

Water trickled over the sides of the birdbath, falling softly over the hyacinths blooming underneath, and the leaves on the lemon tree rustled as a finch fluttered between its branches.

As she waited for the visitor, Tabitha scanned the yard again, to see if everything was in order for their gathering. The tables near the kitchen entrance were set for the midday meal, shaded by her fruit trees. In the afternoon hours, the exterior walls of her villa would shade much of this courtyard as well.

All was ready for the community to arrive after the Rhapsodies' sewing hours were complete.

Glykera stepped into the courtyard, the shadow of a figure lurking in the vestibule behind her. Tabitha tilted her head to see the visitor, a nervous smile on her lips. If it was Matthias, she would remain calm. While he could be quite extravagant with his emotions, he wouldn't want her to be emotional in front of these women.

The shadow stepped into the light, but instead of Matthias, Korinna moved onto the cobbled path between the trees and patches of herbs, her braided brown hair resting over one shoulder. She wore the same tunic as yesterday, ragged and torn at the hem.

Tabitha's smile fell but only for a moment. Standing, she smiled again, arms outstretched as she hurried across the courtyard, grateful to see this young woman again.

"Welcome to our group." Tabitha led her to a divan under the peristyle so they could enjoy the sea air without blistering their skin in the sun, and Korinna scanned the room, her eyes skittering like a frightened animal about to flee.

Tabitha quickly retrieved a second needle from her basket, one made from bronze, as she eyed the tear near the bottom of Korinna's tunic. "Have you ever used a needle?"

"Never," Korinna whispered.

"Why don't we start our sewing lessons by fixing your robe?" Tabitha pointed at the tear. "Then we can begin working on a practice tunic."

Korinna took the needle willingly, and Tabitha showed her how to slip the thread through the loop and knot the end of it between her fingers. She lifted Korinna's skirt and demonstrated how to stitch the two pieces of ragged material together, making what had been torn whole again.

Korinna tried it, then edged her fingers across the repaired ridge. "It's still rough."

Tabitha eyed the young woman's work. "It looks perfect to me."

With those words, she saw a glint of hope in Korinna's eyes, as if this simple act had stitched up something inside her as well.

Tabitha kissed her cheek. "You will make an excellent seamstress and an excellent wife."

Korinna glanced at the birdbath. "I don't want to be Agathon's wife."

Tabitha's heart felt as if it might rip in two. "I wish I could rescue you from this marriage...."

The woman shook her head. "No one can rescue me."

Tabitha reached into her basket and pulled out a coarse piece of wool. A practice square. "I know someone who loves to rescue men and women alike," she said. "Not from a marriage, perhaps, but from something more important."

Korinna blinked. "What can be more important?"

"He can rescue you from the guilt and shame of anything you've ever done wrong in your life, Korinna. He offers salvation to both you and me from our sin."

Korinna's green eyes widened like waters in a pool. "Who is this person who can rescue a slave?"

"His name is Jesus, the Messiah. The Son of God."

"Which god?" she whispered.

"Elohim. The one true God."

Korinna scanned the women sewing nearby. When she didn't respond, Tabitha continued. "This man healed people of their sickness and cast evil spirits out of those being tormented. He even raised two people from the dead."

Korinna shivered, rubbing the mended material between her thin fingers again.

"Even so, many people still didn't believe Him. He angered so many of the religious leaders in Jerusalem that they did something horrific."

Korinna leaned closer. "What did they do?"

"They crucified Him."

When Korinna gasped, several of the women looked their way. Tabitha reassured them with a smile, and they returned to their work.

She remembered so clearly that day Isaac had returned from Jerusalem, devastated at what he'd seen. He had heard Jesus speak months earlier and his life had been changed, but then he recounted how he'd watched as Roman soldiers had nailed the man he thought to be God on a tree. And Isaac saw Mary, a beautiful woman who'd mothered Jesus, kneeling in front of the cross watching her Son die, her heart as broken as His body. She had remained there in dignified strength, bringing Him honor while so many others fled.

"They crucified Jesus and buried Him"—Tabitha pressed a needle through her fabric—"but we learned later He didn't stay in His tomb! Three days after Jesus died, He rose from that grave. The guards found the stone rolled away, His body gone."

Korinna shook her head. "That's impossible."

"That's what the believers in Jerusalem thought, but—"

"Someone must have stolen His body," Korinna insisted.

The exact words Tabitha had spoken when Isaac told her this news, long before she believed.

"Jesus appeared to many different people who had chosen to follow Him," Tabitha said. "And He left them with a gift."

Korinna leaned forward. "How could they possibly have known it was Him?"

Tabitha held out her wrists. "The scars."

The price He'd paid to give them life.

Even after all these years of knowing and believing, the thought of those scars brought tears to her eyes. The price this man had paid, to rescue her and Isaac and this dear young woman sitting beside her, still overwhelmed her. He'd suffered greatly, but in His suffering, Jesus had conquered death itself. A gift like no other.

"After we finish our sewing, a community of His disciples meets here in the courtyard to eat and sing and then discuss Jesus's teachings. You are welcome to join us."

Korinna's gaze fell back to the repaired fabric. "Agathon is expecting me at home."

"Perhaps we can send a message that I've invited you to dine," Tabitha said. "I suspect he will be escorting his cargo up to Jerusalem this afternoon."

Korinna nodded. "He will be staying there for several days."

"Simon the Tanner explains the Gospel much better than I do during these meetings." Tabitha smiled. "But he doesn't know a thing about sewing—"

"Will you really teach me how to make a tunic?"

"Indeed." She broke the woolen thread from Korinna's needle with her teeth and then held up the spool of white thread spun by another widow friend in Joppa. "With this and a bit of fabric, you can create anything you'd like to wear. And you can earn a living with this skill or simply keep your fingers and mind from becoming idle."

"Agathon doesn't allow idleness in our home."

"I suppose that is one thing that Agathon and I might be able to agree upon."

# CHAPTER SIX

The inside of Basil's Inn was dim in this morning hour, the shutters closed. Tabitha had never visited this dingy place, but she'd seen men—and sometimes women—frequent it. The wealthier travelers stayed with friends or family, so this inn near the shore was geared toward sailors and those salesmen who brought goods, like her fabrics, from afar.

Two men, each with the long hair of boatmen, sat out back in the courtyard, drinking from goblets of cheap wine made from the sap of palm trees. An aged woman with blue kohl-lined eyes, brass trinkets dangling from her bracelets, and graying plaits of hair was trying to entertain them with a dance, but the sailors were laughing at her attempts. Their laughter made Tabitha's stomach roll. She wanted to offer this woman hope, a smile even, but the kohl eyes were ablaze in jealousy at the entrance of a new woman. As if Tabitha was trying to steal her clientele.

More than ten thousand residents lived in Joppa, and Tabitha had spent yesterday afternoon roaming through the city, checking the inns, but the boatmen seemed to be sleeping after their journey. A dreadful headache resulted from her futile search, so she'd returned home to sip Glykera's cinnamon tea and close herself off in the darkness of her chamber until it subsided.

Her search continued this morning as she studied the faces of these two sailors who seemed to make sport of wine consumption after their journey. She'd never understood the need to travel, not after roaming for several years across Israel with her uncle. Once Isaac brought her to Joppa, to get away from the uncle who kept asking them for money they didn't have, she never wanted to leave this beautiful port. Joppa was home until Adonai called her to the next life.

When one of the men saw her, he held out his goblet, the clay vessel rocking in his hand. "More wine!" he demanded.

Tabitha took the goblet, the remaining drops of liquid splashing against the sides, but instead of searching for a place to fill it, she sat beside the sailor.

He stopped laughing. "I asked for more wine."

"And I will get you more if—" She leaned toward him. "If you answer a question."

The woman stopped dancing and glared at her, seemingly confused. Then her brass bracelets clanged in frustration with her departure.

"What question?" The words seemed to slosh around the sailor's mouth like the wine in his glass.

"I'm looking for my—" Tabitha stopped. These men who traveled, they all had families. Were they all trying to escape from home? "I'm looking for a boatman named Matthias. Do you know him?"

"Of course I know him."

"Where is he?"

"I don't know." The man belched. "I heard he wouldn't get off the boat."

Her heart soared for just a moment—Matthias had returned—but then it plunged.

"Do you know why?" she asked, trying to control the tremble in her voice.

The sailor shrugged. "Something about his mother."

"His mother…"

He stared down at the goblet in her hand. "I answered your first question and then another."

Tabitha stood and walked slowly toward the small courtyard. A woman was cooking over the fire, and Tabitha handed the goblet to her before rushing outside, back down to the shore. Then she swiftly climbed up onto the rocks of the breakwater and studied the stamp of cedar on the horizon, the ship that her husband had built. The ship her son now used as a refuge like it was the belly of a giant fish in this sea.

Matthias was on the doorstep of Joppa, but he refused to step back into what she prayed was the Lord's plan for his life. And he refused to see her. He'd been abandoned as a child, and now he was abandoning the one who had rescued him, as if this would free him from the chains of his past.

If only she hadn't yelled at him before he left Joppa.

If only she'd told him that she loved him one more time.

If only she'd been able to stop him before he destroyed himself.

Warm wind brushed over her skin, tangling her hair. Her heart felt like stone, anchoring her to the rocks. Matthias was within sight of home, but the boy who'd fought to finish whatever he'd started didn't want to finish his journey back to her. And she had no way now to convince him. Or tell him that she was sorry.

*They that go down to the sea in ships, that do business in great waters; these see the works of the Lord, and his wonders in the deep.… They cry unto the Lord in their trouble, and he bringeth them out of their distresses. He maketh the storm a calm, so that the waves thereof are still.*

The lyrics of this redemptive psalm wafted like perfume through the ocean spray, her mind wandering back to the days after she brought Matthias home. She'd cleansed his body with salt, wrapped him in clean swaddling clothes, and hired a nursemaid, a young woman named Diane, to feed him.

He was clearly Greek with his vibrant blue eyes, but Tabitha knew of no Greek mother who had lost a child. Each time she inquired about a family for adoption, her heart ached at the thought of giving him up. Her closest friends at the time thought she was foolish, that she was trying to use the child to mask the pain of losing her husband. Instead of condemning her, Isaac's church community had surrounded her with support as she'd grown to love the boy.

When Matthias was about ten months old, a wealthy woman from Caesarea offered to raise him as a servant in her home. It would have been a good position for an orphan, Tabitha supposed, but when the time came to make the exchange, she couldn't let him go. That afternoon she'd walked straight to the magistrate and asked about adoption.

With a simple decree, she'd become a mother. Matthias her son.

By the end of that day, nineteen years ago, they were a family, and most families cared for each other for life.

Her uncle hadn't cared one bit about what happened to Tabitha after her mother died. He'd taken her out of obligation, traveling with her from town to town while he sold fine linen from Galilee. She'd been a burden to him—he'd reminded her of that regularly—but he'd given her a gift. Two actually. He had taught her how to negotiate a sale, and he'd waited until Isaac asked to marry her instead of giving her away to a man who would have abused her as his wife.

She scanned the shoreline, looking for a lighter or fishing boat. Perhaps she could hire someone to take her out to the ship. The ropes would be impossible for her to climb, but perhaps Matthias would come down, at least to speak with her.

But if he refused to return home, when his boat sat at the door of Joppa, he probably wouldn't give her an audience there either. If he felt threatened, he'd never come back. The thought of it, losing him for good, felt like a spike driven straight through her heart.

She had never, ever wanted Matthias to feel like a burden. After she adopted him, she'd stumbled her way through motherhood, but they had become a family. Isaac's reputation as a quality shipbuilder had grown rapidly over the years of their marriage, and he'd left her enough money to provide for a son he didn't know he had along with the regular income from Agathon. While Matthias was in school, she had cultivated her passion for sewing and begun opening her home for their church community to meet.

As the years passed, her heart began to change. Adonai had used her son to teach her about His great love and the salvation of the Messiah, just as Adonai must have given Mary the courage that she needed to watch her Son die. Only He could give Tabitha the strength to continue loving others even when it seemed she had lost her son to this world. And He could give Matthias the courage to face the fears that raged inside him, to embrace the love that God—that she—wanted to lavish on him.

Clouds were building over the water as several fishing boats paddled toward the harbor. She'd already missed most of her morning with the Rhapsodies. The noon meal would begin soon for their community, and then the followers would worship in her courtyard. She needed to return home to worship with them today.

Perhaps one of the sailors would deliver a letter to Matthias when the men returned to their ship. She would pour out her heart onto papyrus, asking his forgiveness. Maybe he would come back when Agathon returned again.

Another woman stood by the shore now, probably in her seventies. At least thirty years older than Tabitha. Her tunic was torn like Korinna's, the stains muddying what might have been an ivory color, or perhaps a light tan. Her graying hair was tangled in knots on her head, unadorned with trinkets or beads. Instead of kohl, the circles that lined her eyes seemed to be stained with the same brown from her tunic.

The woman's gaze was focused on the broken bones of a ship that had run aground on the reef years ago, listed to one side, the surge of waves perforating its ribbed planks. The look on her face—it was as if she'd lost someone she loved as well.

Tabitha knew most of her nearest neighbors, by sight if not name, but she didn't recognize this woman. Perhaps she was just passing through.

Even in her sadness, Tabitha could not ignore this woman, a widow, perhaps, in need. After wiping her tears on her sleeve, she slipped up beside her.

"Are you from Joppa?" Tabitha asked.

The woman shook her head, her eyes still focused on the sea.

"But you know someone here—"

"My sister lives nearby."

Was she telling the truth or was she trying to save her dignity?

Either this sister didn't have the means—or desire—to help, or this woman was one of the widows who wandered through the coastal villages, searching for food designated for the rubbish pile or the herd of pigs kept outside the city limits.

Tabitha eyed the woman's hands, to see if she could learn to sew, but her fingers were curled from the stiffness that plagued many women as they climbed in years. Instead of teaching her to sew, Tabitha wanted to help return dignity to this woman in the only other way she knew.

"I'm Tabitha." She nodded toward the water. "I lost a husband to this sea, and now, I fear, I have lost my son."

The woman didn't look her way, but she spoke softly in response. "It's a devastating blow to lose a son."

"What is your name?" Tabitha asked.

Wrinkles around the woman's eyes creased as if she were trying to decide if she could trust a stranger with this information.

Tabitha shook her head. "You don't have to tell me."

"It's Ianthe," she replied, her eyes still on the broken ship. "After my mother."

"Please wait here, Ianthe." Tabitha glanced at the *Chiron* one more time. "I need to retrieve something from my home."

Turning from the salty breeze, she began the hike up to her villa, but her breath seemed to war against this climb, her legs wanting to move faster than her lungs.

Strange—she'd heard others complain of this shortness of breath, but she'd never experienced it before. The sadness, the loss, seemed to be weighing heavily on body and mind.

Instead of entering the front door, Tabitha rushed through an alley behind her house, to the kitchen door. Glykera answered the knock, her apron splattered with sauce.

"Did you find Matthias?" Glykera asked as Tabitha joined her in the kitchen. One of Glykera's granddaughters was preparing the noon meal for their church gathering by scooping fermented fish sauce and stew into bowls for their guests to dip flatbread.

When Tabitha shook her head, the sadness rested between them. Glykera loved Matthias like he was one of her children.

Glykera nodded toward the opposite door, the one that led out into the open courtyard. "They are waiting for you."

Tabitha glanced into the courtyard. Korinna wasn't there, but the rest of the Rhapsodies mingled among the thirty or so people who belonged to their house church. A table before them was filled with dates, sweet chestnuts, and olives the community brought to share.

"Before I join them"—Tabitha turned back to Glykera—"I must take a gift to a new friend."

"Of course," Glykera said, knowing that Tabitha often delivered garments to people across Joppa and the neighboring seaside villages.

Upstairs, in a chamber designed for Isaac's work, a dozen tunics were folded into the beech trunk that he'd made before they married, an object on which to practice his woodworking skills before he started applying them to vessels that now crossed the sea. Tears wet her cheeks again as she smoothed her hands over his carvings of a ship and one of a noble centaur. She opened the trunk, then thumbed through the neatly folded garments, the colors inside as varied as the rays from a setting sun.

Sewing had been her respite since Isaac died as she tried to find her place in a new world without a husband, as a mother who'd never given birth. The sewing kept her hands and mind focused on something besides grief. As she stitched, God had slowly repaired the wounds inside her.

Even now, searching for a tunic in this storage room, her fingers ached to sew again. She couldn't make Matthias return, but she could create something beautiful with her needle and thread, a garment for someone else to wear. A gift rooted from the desperation that spilled out on linen and wool.

She found the perfect tunic for Ianthe, a linen garment made from the green of an unripened olive, an earthy color to hide the relentless mud stains from the shore. A gift of dignity far more prized than the actual fabric in her hands. Priceless, she prayed, for this woman.

In that quiet space, as her church gathered below, Tabitha prayed a blessing over the tunic and anointed it with a drop of myrrh. After draping the material over her arm, she closed the trunk and rushed out of her home and down to the shore where she found Ianthe still waiting by the breakwater.

Tabitha held out the tunic. "I'd like you to have this."

The woman eyed the green linen as if it were a serpent's skin. "I can't take that."

"But I made it," Tabitha insisted. "And I've been wanting to find it a home."

Ianthe lifted her gaze, and Tabitha could see the doubt in her eyes. Suspicion. This woman, she suspected, had been hurt before from the feigned generosity of strangers.

"Why would you give this to me?" Ianthe asked.

Tabitha smiled, her own sorrow lessening in this moment of sharing with someone else who'd known great pain. "Because God loved me so much that He gave me a gift, the greatest gift of all, and I want to give from the depths of His goodness."

She told Ianthe about the church meeting at her home, about the noon meal already prepared, a meal that was served three days a week to anyone who wanted to join them in their worship.

The woman declined the offer of food and worship, but she thanked Tabitha tentatively as she took the tunic. Then she disappeared into one of the winding streets that led back up their hill.

Tabitha prayed that Ianthe would wear the garment instead of selling it. That the blessing would continue on with her.

She glanced out at the *Chiron* one more time.

God had given her more than one gift. He'd given her an entire community who cared for her, and it was time to join her brothers and sisters at home.

# CHAPTER SEVEN

The whispers of singing and the steady beat of a tambourine threaded through the narrow street in front of Tabitha's villa. When she stepped inside again, into the vestibule this time, music flooded from the courtyard. Her friends were singing the psalm about the *tabitha*—*gazelle* in Aramaic—panting for water, their souls longing for their Lord.

That described her, panting like a creature in desperate need of water, except it felt like the river before her had gone dry. She desperately needed sustenance with others who followed Christ.

Dozens in Joppa had faltered in their faith after failing to experience the miracles that the Messiah had done across Israel. No one, to her knowledge, had been healed from a physical ailment in Joppa, but many had been healed on the inside. Those who gathered this afternoon knew He was here because they had experienced the Spirit of God moving in their hearts.

Simon stood in front of the room with his wife and son-in-law, the worshippers fanning out across the courtyard on portable mats as Bethany led them in song, strumming the melody on a lyre to accompany their psalm. Standing near the back, under the fig tree, were Zoe and her son, David.

Tabitha searched the space for Korinna, but she didn't see the young woman. Perhaps Agathon had returned home early from Jerusalem. Or perhaps her words about a Messiah had driven the younger woman away.

She scooted past the chickens gathered in a cluster and stepped up beside Zoe. Her friend reached for her hand, and Tabitha clung to it for strength.

It was hard enough not knowing where Matthias was. How could she tell her friend that Matthias was in Joppa's harbor but refused to return home? Her heart ached like the day Isaac had died, except her husband never meant to leave her.

"We missed you this morning," Zoe whispered.

"I had to inquire again about Matthias."

"And?"

Tabitha simply shook her head.

David looked up at his mother. "Are you well, Imma?"

"I am fine." Zoe kissed her son's forehead, then squeezed Tabitha's hand before releasing it to hold David's.

Bethany began leading them in a new song. Closing her eyes, the melody settling inside her, Tabitha remembered the depth of Matthias's passion for this woman who led them in worship today. Even if he returned home, how could he possibly make it right again with Simon and Bethany and the others?

"We have a letter from Peter," Simon said, holding up a scroll. "God has used him to heal a paralyzed man in Lydda."

A murmur rippled across the room, excitement over this miracle and anticipation to hear what this apostle would teach them next. They were all hungry, not just for the meal they'd eat together, but for words to feed their souls.

Lydda was only a day's journey from here, and they all hoped Peter would meet with Joppa's community soon to answer their many questions and bolster their faith.

Simon opened the scroll.

"I greet each of you in the name of our Lord Jesus Christ," he read. "I'm told you have lived well together as Hebrew brothers and sisters who honor His name."

Another murmur, and Tabitha thought those behind her were reacting to Peter's words since many Greek men and women like Simon's family worshipped here alongside those who were Hebrew. But then David turned his head and tugged on his mother's hand. When Zoe turned around, she gasped.

"Tabitha—" Zoe whispered.

Her heart pounded, but her eyes remained on Simon, whose words had faded away, his eyes narrowing.

Was it possible that Matthias had returned home after all?

She couldn't turn around. Not yet. Couldn't bear another disappointment.

David was the one who answered her question.

"Matthias!" he shouted, running between Tabitha and his mother, toward the man he used to follow around.

Tabitha finally turned and saw the sight she'd been longing for. Matthias was at the back of the courtyard, watching her.

Her heart tumbled and she no longer cared what he thought about her emotion. Or what anyone else in that room thought of her. She rushed forward like David, arms outstretched.

Finally, her son had come home.

Matthias stepped back as the familiar faces around the court-yard stared at him. Everything within him screamed *run*, but he fought the urge to race out the door and paddle back to the refuge—the fortress—of his ship.

"I'm only here for the day," he explained to his mother.

"But you are here," she said, clinging to his arm, tears streaming down her face. "That's all that matters now."

Imma had aged in the past year, grooves sinking deeper into her forehead, red eyes that mirrored the agony in his heart. For so long he'd been afraid to see her again, afraid of the condemnation in her eyes, but he saw no condemnation in them now. Only love, pouring out.

Bethany stood near the front of the room, just as beautiful as when he'd seen her the night of her wedding, but he only got a glimpse before Joshua stepped in front of his bride. As if Matthias might sprint across the room and steal her away.

Matthias took another step back. "I shouldn't have interrupted—"

"Of course you should have," Tabitha insisted.

He'd spent much of his youth in these meetings, although in his later years, he'd been more focused on Bethany than the words of her father or anyone else who spoke.

Glykera stole up beside them, the woman who had been much more like an auntie to him than a servant. "Welcome home!"

He kissed her cheek. "You are a beautiful sight for these eyes."

Glykera tsked. "I am drawing a bath for you right away."

"Some find the smell of sea to be soothing," he said, smiling at her.

"It's nothing but stench to me."

Imma wiped back her tears. "You can bathe when you're ready."

"Matthias." Simon stepped up to him. "Why have you returned?"

A fire sparked inside him, and he clenched his fists together, trying to stop its roar in the face of this man he despised. He had just as much right, more even, to be in his home. The place where he was supposed to belong. "I've come to see my mother."

Simon eyed him warily. "And no one else?"

His gaze wandered again to Bethany near the far wall, her delicate lips pressed together, her head bowed as if her heart had been broken like his. Joshua glared back at him, his hand against his wife's back.

Matthias wished he could throw one more punch, this time to erase the smirk from that man's face.

Matthias turned back to Simon. "There is no one else left to see."

Joshua escorted Bethany away, probably escaping out the kitchen door. Simon's entire family, he suspected, would disappear until Matthias left again for Greece.

He'd seen enough scoundrels in his travels. He didn't need to immerse himself again into a community that wounded its members. Hypocrites, that's what a rabbi would have called this community. People who followed God with their lips but not with their actions.

His mother and Bethany and the women from her sewing group were the exceptions. They, it seemed, were the only ones intent on serving Elohim.

If only he could speak with Bethany one more time—

Several women greeted him, said they were glad he was home, and through the agonizing minutes that followed, neither Imma nor young David left his side.

His mother was the best sailor Matthias knew, riding with him for a lifetime through every storm, anchoring him when necessary until he jumped overboard. Even now, after his shipwreck of a life, she was still on board.

The worshippers began to disperse, returning to their work for the afternoon. He greeted Zoe before she gently pried David away from him.

"Are you hungry?" Imma asked.

"Always."

"We'll have a feast for dinner."

"After he takes a bath," Glykera interjected.

He smiled again. "After a bath…"

But even as he cleansed his skin with the strigil and shaved off his beard, his mind returned to the beautiful woman who'd been playing the lyre as he waited in the vestibule, who had smiled at him before her husband blocked her view. Simon, her father, had treated Matthias as if he were dirt to be scraped off his sandal.

Was Bethany happy in her marriage to Joshua?

As he soaked in the bath, he wondered again if she still longed for him like he did for her.

He leaned back in the water, enjoying its warmth after the windy breezes on the lighter. None of the women he'd met in Athens compared to her.

The smile on Bethany's face, her voice that soothed the worry in his dreams. He'd tried to block out these memories of her over the past year, but they kept returning.

If only he could go back in time, he would change everything.

# CHAPTER EIGHT

Tabitha lowered the needle, a silver thread trailing across her tunic. As Matthias bathed, her hands needed to stay busy, the blood rushing through her skin so rapidly that they trembled. The emotions of the week tumbled inside her, and her fingers wouldn't cooperate with the stitching.

The dark blue linen in her lap, the silver thread in her fingers, reminded her of the evening sky dotted with stars. A thousand possibilities.

If only she could orchestrate the future for those she loved.

As Glykera prepared their dinner meal, Tabitha wished she could throw a homecoming banquet for her son, but most everyone in her community, except Zoe and David and a few old friends, were afraid of what Matthias might do. Even today, when he'd arrived during the service, the wild look in his eyes made her worry that he would hide like a hyrax before she could welcome him home.

He'd decided to come during worship, she guessed, so that words would be few between them. She didn't need many words. Instead she'd enjoy his company for the hours that he would give her, knowing he might leave just as quickly as he'd come.

She lifted her needle again, pushed it through the linen, and pulled it out on the other side. Then she lowered the material back to her lap, the stitch crooked. If she kept working like this, she'd ruin the garment meant to replace the one she'd given to Ianthe. While she had enough income to provide for her household, wasting it would benefit none of them.

God had given her this heart desire to see Matthias one more time. She would be strong for the remainder of the afternoon. No more tears that might prompt him to run away.

Long shadows swept through the window when she joined Glykera in the kitchen. The evening meal preparations were finished. On the counter rested a platter with the remaining lamb along with fig preserves, flatbread, and ceramic bowls filled with sauces and lentil stew.

And Matthias still hadn't emerged from the private chamber that held a latrine and tub.

Tabitha glanced toward the curtain at the far side of the kitchen. "Do you think he's preparing to leave tonight?"

"No," Glykera said, her arms covered in fine flour. "I think he's afraid."

Tabitha leaned back against the wooden counter. "You raised five children, and none of them have left Joppa."

"Two of them wanted to," Glykera replied. "They just didn't have an opportunity."

Tabitha lifted the platter. "I want to be a better mother." Like the mothers who had birthed their children. All these years had passed, and she still had much to learn.

"You're already a good mother," Glykera said. "One day both you and Matthias will realize it."

As the time passed, the warm water Glykera brought for Matthias's bath had turned a pleasant cool. He hadn't bathed in fresh water since he'd visited the bathhouse in Athens, several weeks past, so he scrubbed every bit of spray and dirt from his skin before soaking in his thoughts.

Glykera had draped a clean tunic and cord over the side of a chair, a garment that his mother had made him. One that he'd left behind with most of his things when he'd fled. His traveling garment, he guessed, was either soaking in a tub of its own or had been sent up to burn in the dump where Imma had found him long ago.

A curtain covered the entrance into this room, and the only window was a slit above the tub. The light had begun to fade when he finally dried off. Then he dressed in the waiting tunic and combed back his long hair.

Still, he hesitated. Nothing was rocking in this room, no storms battering the sides of their villa, and yet he still felt as if he might topple.

Someone stepped up to the curtain, toes slipping underneath the edge. "Matthias?" Glykera called.

He couldn't hide any longer.

"I'm dressed," he said as he strung his purse through the cord around his waist.

She pulled the curtain open. "Come eat dinner with your mother."

"I'm tired…."

Glykera settled one hand into the folds of her hip, leaning into it. "Why did you come home, Matthias?"

He tied the cord. "The captain sent me ashore to load the new cargo."

"And you had no place else to go."

"I wanted to see Imma and all of you. I was just—"

"Scared." Glykera finished the sentence for him.

Perhaps he was scared, but he wouldn't admit it.

"You are a man now, one who has seen the world," she said. "I'd hoped you would have realized by now that no one in this world cares for you more than that woman waiting to dine with you."

A trembling deep teetered between what was safe and what terrified him. "I know."

"So stop chasing after everything and everyone else and go enjoy what you have."

He nodded but didn't move.

Glykera folded her arms. "Did you forget your way?"

"No." A smile crawled up his face. "I'm just wondering how I ended up with two mothers."

Glykera swatted him, and he hurried down the hall. When he reached the kitchen, she handed him a plate with cheese and he carried it outside. Lanterns hung on columns around the courtyard, and two low tables were laden with bowls of food and stone goblets waiting to be filled, the aroma of roasted lamb spiced with mint filling the air.

Imma rose from one of the cushions that surrounded the tables and reached out her hands to squeeze both of his. "I'm glad you're home, Son."

"I'm glad as well."

Glykera filled the goblets with diluted wine, and they each washed their hands in a basin of water. Then Glykera, along with her husband, reclined on cushions to enjoy this meal with Matthias and his mother, passing around bowls of food in which to dip their flatbread.

Niles scooped up a mixture of ground chestnuts and oil. "Tell us about your journey,"

Matthias reached for a cluster of grapes. As they ate, he entertained them with stories about the storms they'd encountered on the water, about getting lost after they'd left the island of Cyprus, and about the sea monster that stalked them before they arrived in Greece.

Glykera leaned forward when he talked about this monster. "A *ketos?*"

"Perhaps. We only saw glimpses of the creature in the fog, as if it was waiting for the winds to topple us."

Glykera shivered, but neither Niles nor Imma seemed to believe his story. He'd never actually seen the creature, but the other sailors swore this mythical monster had preyed on their ship.

Niles grinned as he reached for a piece of lamb. "Was there a nymph riding on it?"

Matthias shook his head. "It was completely untamed."

"Sort of like the sailors."

Tabitha leaned toward the table. "What was Athens like?"

"More beautiful than I ever imagined and crowded with people from all over the world." He didn't tell them about the women he'd encountered, the gods that demanded allegiance, or the doubts he'd had in the midst. "The Parthenon was like a beacon from the sea."

They knew about the famous temple on the acropolis, built for the goddess Athena, but none seemed to be intrigued by it.

A battle had raged inside him during those months in Greece, and he'd wished that he could sift through all the stories, the overwhelming rhetoric, and discover the truth. Several years ago, he'd heard a man in Jerusalem speak confidently, like his mother and Simon, about the resurrection of those who were dead in spirit and in body, but to him the resurrection of the Hebrew man named Jesus was just as outlandish as the stories of the nymphs and sea monsters.

As the night air cooled, Niles stole back to the kitchen and Glykera refilled their wine goblets before joining her husband. Matthias and his mother rested quietly beside the table, their stomachs content. And he was glad that he had come, if only to find some peace inside him from the rocking.

"How long will the *Chiron* be here?" Imma asked.

"Probably until the end of the week. The captain is anxious to return to Greece."

"Perhaps you can stay here until everything is loaded…."

He shook his head. "I'll be leaving in the morning."

"To sleep on the ship?"

"Wherever they need me."

His mother glanced at one of the lights flickering nearby before looking back at him. "I must ask you something, Matthias."

He bristled, thinking of the many things that she might want him to do. But he was a man now, one with respectable work. He didn't answer to anyone now except the captain and only when he wanted.

She leaned toward the table, her voice quiet. "Will you please forgive me?"

Her words warred within him, for she had done nothing wrong. He was the one who'd left without saying goodbye.

"Why would I need to forgive you?" he finally asked.

"For not loving you the way I should have when you were younger." Her voice cracked. "For not understanding the pain you must have endured as a child."

He shook his head. "You loved me more than anyone has ever loved me. You gave me everything I needed."

"I'm sorry for yelling at you that night you left."

That awful night he wished he could erase from all of their minds. "I forgave you long ago."

"Then why didn't you want to come home?" Even though her gaze was strong, he could hear the ache in her voice.

He reached for his goblet and took a long sip. "Glykera thinks I was afraid."

"Are you?" When he shrugged, she scooted to the edge of her divan. "Are you afraid of me?"

He took a deep breath, his confidence bolstered by the wine. "It wasn't you that I feared."

But even as he said the words, he knew they weren't entirely true. He wasn't afraid of his mother's actions, but he feared what she thought of him. That he had disappointed her beyond repair. "I've changed in this past year."

"We all have changed."

"At the wedding—"

She reached for his hand. "I believe Simon's family will forgive you, if only you'd ask."

"Forgive me?"

"Please, Matthias."

"But I didn't do anything wrong!" Simon and Joshua had wronged him, and both men had gotten exactly what they deserved.

His mother studied him for a moment as if she could see all that was bubbling inside him, about to erupt onto the remains of the banquet between them. Perhaps she feared that she might never be able to clean up the mess, because she deftly changed the topic. "What if you stayed home?"

"I'm not planning to stay—"

"You could resume your work at the market," she continued. "The Rhapsodies and I would much rather sew the tunics than sell them."

He leaned back against the cushion, considering her words. He would never forgive Simon, but perhaps he didn't need to leave Joppa forever. He had enjoyed the negotiating, the selling of the garments, the knowing their profits were returning to women who needed the money. And when Joshua was out fishing, Bethany would surely come to buy wares for their home. He could see her in the market.

Many of the women he'd met in Athens had divorced and married again or remained without a husband so they could entertain more than one man. Under Hebrew law, a woman couldn't divorce her husband, but a man could divorce his wife.

"I've promised Agathon that I would return to Greece one more time."

Her smile was tentative as if she feared to hope. "You could help us sell our wares when you return."

Perhaps it wasn't too late for him and Bethany if Joshua gave her a proper divorce. Matthias would simply rescue her from a marriage that had broken them both, and Simon could do nothing to stop them.

When he came back to Joppa, he and Bethany could form a plan.

Perhaps then his world would stop rocking around him.

# CHAPTER NINE

The grass around the cavern was overgrown, the area rarely grazed by goats or crushed by the heels of someone else climbing up the hill to say goodbye to their loved one who'd been buried behind the stone.

The scent from her garden roses, the bouquet clutched in her hands, carried Tabitha out of Joppa and back up this ridge. Isaac's spirit didn't linger in this grove, but she still returned often, as if by talking to the legacy of her husband, she might glean his wisdom.

Creamy white flowers blossomed on the olive trees, their petals snowing down before scattering across the grass. From up here, she could see the hull of the *Chiron* waiting for her men to sail her back to Greece. Waiting to take Matthias away again.

Her son had stayed at home longer than a night. Four nights had passed as they'd waited for Agathon's caravan to return with its merchandise from Jerusalem. Now the man was back in Joppa with cartloads of supplies to fill his ship.

Early this morning, Matthias had left to help the other crewmen load these wares, a process that could take an entire week depending on the weather. When he wasn't loading the crates, she planned to savor every hour they had left together.

The skies had been clear since Matthias had returned, but summer often carried with it the threat of fog or even a thunderstorm. Was it wrong to pray for storms? Just a little rain to keep her son home a few hours, even a day or two longer. The lure of Athens, she feared, would cage him and keep him trapped there for the rest of his life.

She arranged the flowers in front of the cave before leaning back against a knobbed olive branch, her heart aching with memories.

"Mathias is a fine man," she said, no one but the birds to hear the words meant for her late husband. "Stubborn like me when he's angry, but there's a kindness underneath that thick skin. And a heart that's been broken." A heart only the Spirit of their Lord could mend.

Under Isaac's tutelage, Matthias might have become a shipbuilder or even a ship owner. Isaac would have helped him embrace a trade while channeling all of his passion into productive work.

"You would have been proud of him."

She stopped to listen, as if Isaac might respond. Finches sang overhead in the olive branches, and she soaked in heaven's choir. Trumpeters, some of these birds were called, spreading their music across the arid lands of Israel.

One bird interrupted the melody with a squawk, and she closed her eyes for a moment, listening to its cry. The one bird who wouldn't sing with the others.

Glykera and Niles had been riveted by all of Matthias's seafaring tales. The monsters and storms and getting lost among the high waves worried Tabitha, but she really was proud of his ability to tackle these adventures on his own. She'd told him that she loved him, that she wanted him to stay home, but she wouldn't dare say a word in an attempt to scare him away from returning to Greece. Her years of instruction were long over, and any warning from her would only push him over the edge, plunging him fully into whatever Athens and the islands offered him.

So she redirected her voice, asking the Lord for help in guiding this man. Hoping, this time, that God would answer her prayer.

Then she prayed for each of the Rhapsodies. Korinna had yet to return to their group, but Tabitha prayed that once Agathon was gone, she would rejoin them, immersing herself in the hope and peace of Christ as she sewed.

"And for our church," she prayed. "Please give us new opportunities to share the Good News to both Jews and Greeks."

The desire for redemption overflowed inside her, but often it seemed to simply puddle up on the ground. The Jewish people and their Greek neighbors all worked together in Joppa, yet most of them were firmly divided.

Surely God would want all of them to worship together.

She kissed her palm and pressed it against the cold stone, her head beginning its familiar ache after she'd spent too much time in the sun. Matthias said he would join them for dinner, and she'd asked Glykera to prepare a feast. Instead of having him leave again in anger, she wanted to send him off immersed in love, eager to return.

She lingered another moment before turning with the breeze, away from the tree and stone, to begin her own journey home.

When she'd first begun visiting Isaac's grave, she'd taken the traveler's road called *Via Maris*—Way of the Sea—that bypassed the dump, but after finding Matthias, she'd changed her weekly route, walking the perimeter of the refuse pile instead.

This afternoon she circled quietly, listening as she always did for the cries of a child. She'd never discovered another abandoned baby since Matthias, but if a boy or girl were forsaken again, she wanted to hear its cry.

Several people were rummaging through the dump, searching, she supposed, for food or something to reuse or resell in the market. A partially broken vessel, perhaps, or the leather of a sandal or a piece of lost jewelry. Tabitha opened her satchel and removed a napkin filled with shelled almonds. It had been many years since she'd known real hunger, but the pains of it once plagued her—and the memory of it continued to haunt her whenever she saw someone in need.

In her youth Tabitha had vowed that as long as she had the means, she would never allow anyone in her presence to go hungry. She only had the simplest of gifts to offer, tunics and food, but she prayed that God would use them for His good.

She opened the napkin carefully so not a single almond would fall on the dirty ground. One of the scavengers—a woman—stopped digging when she eyed the seeds.

Tabitha held out her hand. "These are for you."

At the invitation, the woman reached out and snatched the almonds as if she feared Tabitha might change her mind. Then she devoured them before returning to her work.

Another woman crept down from the top of the heap, her wares bundled up in the folds of her tunic. Tabitha recognized the olive-green garment the woman wore, one she had stitched with care and then blessed for its new owner. Tabitha waved her hand. "Ianthe!"

The woman glanced up with surprise. Though her graying hair hung ratted around her shoulders and the hem of her garment was now ringed with dust, Tabitha could see the beauty in her desert-brown eyes and the heart of a much younger woman who needed a friend.

"I brought almonds to share," Tabitha said, holding out the remaining seeds.

With one arm Ianthe cradled the bulge she carried in her tunic as she opened her other hand. Tabitha poured the almonds into it.

The woman sniffed the handful then took a bite. "'Tis a gift from the gods."

"A gift from the one God, I believe."

Ianthe studied her as she ate another almond. "Why are you up here?"

It wasn't an easy question to answer, not without sounding like she wanted to be a savior. She was only a watering can to pour out whenever Adonai tipped the spout.

"I come every week"—she pointed back toward the grove—"to visit my husband's grave and ask God for ways to use the life He's given me."

In a world where few widows were respected, their gifts condemned, Tabitha knew it was a lot for this woman to understand.

"God loves you, Ianthe, and He wants to do something beautiful with the rest of your life."

"There's no beauty left...."

"I see plenty of beauty in you."

Ianthe glanced back at the mountain of trash as if she had to decide between the offer of beauty or her reality of ashes. Most widows, in Tabitha's experience, didn't want charity; they wanted opportunities. And they wanted family.

Only God could stitch together a family for people who no longer had one.

"Please come to my house for a meal," Tabitha said, rubbing the sides of her head to relieve some of the pain. "Just for today."

"I don't want to impose on your kindness."

"It would be an honor to have you."

Ianthe released her bundle and the rubbish inside fell to the ground, mixing again with the other forgotten things. And she walked beside Tabitha, around a stately palm tree that overlooked Joppa and down into the neighborhood as if they were truly sisters on their way home.

# CHAPTER TEN

Matthias's limbs ached from a full day of lifting crates from the warehouse and rowing them out to the ship, but his legs weren't sore enough to avoid the detour that he took daily before walking home.

While he'd been told that Bethany and Joshua were living at Simon's villa, he'd yet to see Bethany when he passed by. Still it didn't stop him from checking the windows to see if she might be watching for him. She must know that he would come for her.

Agathon was planning to leave port in three days, once the crew finished loading the goods and stocking food for the voyage down to Alexandria and then a week up to Athens. They'd continue their journey to Malta and Crete, both islands where Agathon could charge three to four times more than he could obtain in Egypt or Greece.

In the hours that Matthias and the other boatmen worked, he had formed a plan. For a passage fee, Agathon would allow Bethany to travel with them. They could either disembark on one of the islands for a season or complete the journey home. When they returned, Joshua would ask for a divorce, and Matthias could help his mother sell her garments, providing a living for him and his wife.

The market stall had been a profitable venture when he and his mother had partnered together before, but they could expand the business significantly. The women in Jerusalem and at ports across the Mediterranean were anxious to mimic the colorful garments of the wealthy. Simon hadn't thought Matthias would be successful, but he would succeed in this profession and provide well for his family.

The possibilities had solidified in his mind since he'd returned home, but he had yet to speak with Bethany. Simon and Joshua had conveniently hidden her away, but the men couldn't keep them apart forever. Somehow he would talk with her before this ship returned to Greece. Together they would concoct a plan.

Agathon, he'd heard, was planning to wed when the *Chiron* returned again. Perhaps they'd only be away for a month or two. If he couldn't speak with Bethany now, they'd find a way to be together after he arrived back at this harbor with extra money in his purse.

His stomach growled, the bread and cheese he'd eaten at noon long forgotten by the time Agathon dismissed them. Ahead was Simon's villa, the front door closed and probably locked. He'd knocked twice already this week, but the servant who'd opened it sent him away without even announcing his visit. And the snarl of a watchdog reiterated the servant's action when he'd tried to reopen the door on his own.

He lingered in these late afternoon hours by the villa as he watched the windows, driven by a different hunger. If only he could catch a glimpse of Bethany, long enough to wave her down to the street so they could talk.

No one passed by the window, but at the end of the lane, resting on the cobblestones, was the woman who'd been the guest of honor at their home last night, an impoverished Greek woman named Ianthe.

Her eyes were closed, her worn head resting back against a stone wall in the shade. To her side was a leather pouch and an alabaster flask with a stopper, the marble edge cracked.

Had she collected these from the dump?

No one had mentioned where Imma met this woman, but he suspected it was above Joppa. Neither pedigrees nor the formalities of an introduction deterred his mother when it came to inviting guests for dinner. She had no trouble asserting herself in the marketplace to sell the wares of her friends or along the street if she saw someone in need.

Last night, after their dinner, Imma had invited Ianthe to sleep in one of the rooms upstairs, but the woman had declined, insisting that she had a mat waiting at her sister's home. Imma said that she was welcome back anytime.

He approached Ianthe warily, wondering if she had collapsed from too much drink.

She sat up quickly when she heard him, her eyes tired but clear. "Matthias?"

He slid down next to her, wishing his mother were here. She would know exactly what to say.

"Are you ill?" he asked.

"I'm well." She straightened her thin shoulders. "Thank you."

He looked both ways on the street, and they were alone. "Do you need a place to spend the night?"

"No," she said. "My sister has a place for me."

Matthias could usually spot a lie a good fathom away, but he wasn't certain whether or not this woman was telling the truth.

"Would you like to join us again for dinner?" he asked.

"My sister—"

"I know. She has a place for you." His mother didn't always know when to leave people alone, but he understood the need for space. He'd stop pestering this woman with questions.

"You're a good son, Matthias," she said. "Tabitha is blessed to have you."

Blessed might not be the word he'd use, but she was very patient with him and he was grateful for it.

The woman smiled as he stood, her lips cushioned around the few teeth that still clung to her gums. "I wish I had a son like you."

For a moment he wanted to put his arms around her and kiss her forehead, but she would surely think him silly.

When he stepped back, she stopped him. "Please wait."

"What is it?"

"I've brought something for your mother's headaches." Ianthe held out the flask. "This tincture will help relieve the pain."

Imma pretended all was well, but he feared the years of work, of care, had instigated her pain. Her heart was just as passionate, her desire to bless all those around her with good, but her body wouldn't keep up with her will.

"What's in the tincture?"

"Elderflower and lavender oils. They're meant to ease any pain."

He took the flask. "I'll give it to her."

When he stepped through the open door at home, into the vestibule, he heard laughter ebbing in from the courtyard. His mother had invited another guest, it seemed, to dinner. That wasn't unusual, but the laughter—he hadn't heard his mother laugh like that in years.

Curious, he slipped through the door and saw Imma under the peristyle, sitting on a divan beside a young woman. When the woman glanced up at him, his mouth gaped open. Her dark plaited hair rested over one shoulder, and her eyes, they were as green as the emeralds he'd seen on display in Greece.

This woman, it seemed, had brought joy back into their home.

Tabitha saw the look in her son's eyes as he entered the courtyard, admiration bronzed into his smile. Korinna had returned for another sewing lesson in the hours after their community had worshipped, and Matthias was intrigued by her friend.

"This is Korinna," she said, introducing them. "We've spent most of our afternoon sewing together."

Matthias nodded but didn't reply. He tried to treat all the women in his mother's group with equal respect, but she recognized that look in his eyes. Resolute as if he were trying to crack open a pomegranate with his hands, desperate for the sweetness inside.

Sweetness that didn't belong to him.

Agathon wouldn't tolerate anyone, especially not Tabitha's son, trying to steal the woman he planned to marry.

"I'd best go home." Korinna lowered the piece of wool to her lap, her gaze traveling to the door near the courtyard.

"Matthias?" Tabitha prompted, and she hoped, in his curiosity, that he wouldn't say anything to wound this young woman. Korinna was like one of the flowers in her small garden, beautiful but delicate. Easy to trample, she feared.

"It's a pleasure to meet you," he finally replied. "But it seems as if we've met before."

She reached for her basket, but she didn't stand.

"You were working for Agathon last year," he continued. "You brought a meal to the ship before we left."

She nodded slowly. "I've been working for Agathon most of my life."

The words settled over them, the weight of their meaning anchoring into the ground. The only reason a woman would have worked in the household as a child was if Agathon had purchased her.

Tabitha was proud of Korinna for taking a risk to come here and learn instead of hiding away in Agathon's house. Proud of her for being honest when the reality was so hard. She might be a slave, but her heart, Tabitha prayed, would be set free.

Matthias nodded at the square of wool. "Are you a member of the Rhapsodies?"

"I've only been to one of their meetings, but your mother has offered to teach me how to sew even when I can't attend."

Tabitha smiled. "She's learning quickly."

"Those ladies seem mild-mannered, but don't let them fool you." Matthias propped his foot up on the edge of the birdbath, his confidence restored. "They are a tenacious group, especially with my mother at the helm."

"You're blessed to have a mother who will fight for those she loves."

Tabitha's heart swelled. She was supposed to be helping this woman, but the words Korinna spoke infused her with life. In the past week, this young woman had captured her heart, just like Matthias had done long ago.

"Indeed," Matthias said, glancing back and forth between the women. "She'll fight to the death if she must."

"A warrior," Korinna said, and Tabitha saw a flicker of a smile on her lips. "Defeating the enemy with her bronze needles instead of a sword."

"A servant," Tabitha insisted, embarrassed at their banter. Her gaze fell, and she saw the cracked vessel in Matthias's hand. "What did you bring home?"

"Some sort of potion from Ianthe." He stepped forward and placed the flask beside her, the sweet scent wafting up. "She says these oils will help cure your headaches, but I'm not entirely sure about the contents."

Had she even told Ianthe about her headaches? She didn't remember speaking about them, but the woman seemed to have been blessed with the gift of intuition. Perhaps she could simply tell that Tabitha's head was hurting, like Tabitha could tell when someone's heart ached.

"I will try her medicine the next time it bothers me." She didn't tell Matthias that the headaches had been coming more frequently now, lest he worry. They would subside, she hoped, when the rainy days returned.

He turned toward Korinna. "Are you joining us for dinner?"

She shook her head, gauging the time by the shadows. "I must go home to help serve our dinner meal."

"Surely Agathon wouldn't mind if you stayed," he said, but Matthias knew—like all of them—that Agathon would mind very much. He would be furious, in fact, if he didn't know the whereabouts of his staff.

Korinna folded the material, leaving it on the divan as she stood. "I must leave."

After Tabitha kissed her cheek, Korinna rushed toward the door. Then Matthias planted himself on the divan, stretching his long legs across the cushions as he closed his eyes, seeming to lose himself in his thoughts.

Stars had begun to rise over the yard. The end to another day with her son. How she wished that she could stuff all of this into a glass jar, keeping the memories of this night forever.

But even as she cherished these moments with Matthias, Korinna was going home to a man who cared nothing for her good. Agathon was well aware of the jealousy of the other men, the power he'd hold, with a wife as beautiful as Korinna by his side. Unlike Simon, who'd tried to reason with Matthias, Agathon would lord Korinna's beauty over the other men. Tempting them before snatching her away. She would be used as a pawn to entice them and then he'd take pleasure in their demise.

Matthias could easily fall prey.

"Agathon is going to marry her when he returns," she said, wanting Matthias to understand this boundary so he wouldn't try to usurp ownership when he had none.

"That poor woman—"

"Agathon would kill you if you tried to stop him."

He opened one eye, glancing back. "I have no desire to do so."

As his mother, she knew him better than anyone, and he was thinking about something—someone else, perhaps—that he should not.

Her head began to hurt again, and she poured several drops from Ianthe's alabaster and rubbed the sweet-smelling tincture under her hairline, the oils taming some of the pain.

No one, man or woman, should be enslaved. To himself or another or to the sin that the world offered.

She wished she could sweep in and rescue Ianthe and Korinna and her son, but only the Messiah could save any of them. Instead she'd pray that they would find freedom through the Son of God, who'd already broken the chains. Set all of them free.

# CHAPTER ELEVEN

Korinna pushed the bronze needle through the lemon-colored fabric. It was a sample piece, a tunic to wear at home. She was supposed to be starting her wedding garment, but she couldn't bear the thought yet of stitching a bridal gown to wear for Agathon. Each time Tabitha mentioned it, Korinna said she still must practice, as if she could delay the ceremony by her lack of a tunic.

The Rhapsodies, all nine of them, laughed together as they worked, peace settling over this courtyard like sea spray on a sun-soaked afternoon. David entertained the women by chasing a chicken through the herb gardens and around the lemon tree. Zoe sat beside Miriam at the birdbath, the two of them like hens themselves, cackling about raising children. Miriam's daughters were grown now, married off to men in other towns, but Zoe mothered well, loving this boy who had no father left to provide for him.

Korinna was too tired to laugh and had nothing to contribute to a conversation about children. Instead she pulled her arms close to her chest, wondering what it would be like to hold a baby of her own. She'd never abandon her child, even if Agathon were the father, but the thought of being with Agathon caused the nausea to whirl inside her again. She'd have no child, boy or girl, without him, but she could never love that man. And she didn't know the first thing about being a wife.

Selene had treated Agathon with respect, loving him even, and he'd been respectful in return. But no matter what Korinna did, Agathon would never respect her like that. Even as his wife, she'd always be a slave in his eyes.

When the chicken raced into the vestibule, David collapsed onto the ground. The women clapped at his endeavor, and she hoped, for Zoe's sake, that he would grow up to care well for his mother.

Tabitha carried out a platter with grapes and goat cheese from the kitchen. Everyone except Korinna put down her sewing to enjoy the midmorning meal.

"Do you think Matthias could sell our garments in the market again?" Miriam asked.

Tabitha was smiling, yet there was a sadness in her smile. "Perhaps when he returns from Greece."

"It's beastly for Agathon to require him to go back out." Miriam looked over at Korinna apologetically.

"I'm not certain that it's a requirement," Tabitha said, but Korinna had heard Agathon talk about Matthias. According to him, Matthias had to sail one more time, to pay back the money he owed.

Tabitha brought a handful of grapes to Korinna. "Please eat something."

"I'm not hungry." It was a lie, but she feared imposing on Tabitha's hospitality. This home had become a safe haven for her. An oasis.

"We don't want it to go to waste."

Tabitha was just being gracious. If Korinna didn't eat the fruit, someone from the church community would enjoy it in the next hour. These disciples of Jesus seemed to enjoy everything. How could they not, she supposed, if their god had truly been raised from the grave. What must it feel like to be redeemed by this man they called the Messiah? To be free.

"Please." Tabitha held the grapes out again, and Korinna's stomach rumbled from hunger. She took the cluster and ate the sweet fruit, the juice reviving her.

"Thank you."

Tabitha reached for her basket and pulled out a piece of linen the color of lilac. "This is dyed by a sister named Lydia."

"I didn't realize you had a sister," Korinna said, fingering the fine material.

"She's my sister in Christ, like all of the women here today."

Except her. She'd never had a sister.

"Is Agathon treating you well?" Tabitha asked.

"Well enough," she replied. "Better than most slaves."

"You might not have a father in this world, but our God loves His children like a father."

Korinna shook her head. "I've never known a father who loves."

"He loves you, Korinna. He'll show you if you'll let Him."

But how could this God of the universe love her? A pagan and an orphan. Not even her master, her future husband, thought she was worth loving. All of the ladies in this group had been loved before they decided to follow Jesus.

"Did you know your parents?" Korinna asked.

Tabitha glanced out at the water spilling over the birdbath. "My father was a Hebrew man, but he died a year after I was born, so I don't remember him. My mother was the most beautiful woman I've ever known. I thought she was a goddess when I was a girl."

"What happened to her?"

"She died when I was fourteen," Tabitha said. "*Carcinos* spilled like ink inside her."

"It's sad to lose a mother."

"Indeed."

Korinna's mind drifted, wondering again what happened to the woman who'd birthed her. She'd never know. Selene had purchased her from a slave market in Cyprus when Korinna was three. No matter what anyone said, she refused to think her parents sold her. Perhaps she'd gotten lost or someone stole her away. Some days she wondered if they were still looking for their daughter.

"Do you remember your parents?" Tabitha asked.

"No."

Tabitha patted her knee. "Not all parents are able to take care of their children as they should, but you can still love a child even when they are far away."

One day she'd love a baby of her own, and she swore by the goddess Leto that nothing would stop her from caring for her future child.

Tabitha held up the linen. "Now we must start on your wedding dress."

The sight of purple, the promise it held, made Korinna's stomach tumble again. "I'd like to begin tomorrow, please."

"Korinna—"

"Tomorrow is soon enough."

Tabitha folded the linen and tucked it back into her basket. "I understand."

Miriam sat down beside them, a lump of red fabric in her lap. "I think it's going to rain."

Tabitha looked up at the clear sky. "How do you know?"

"I can feel it in my bones."

Tabitha turned toward Korinna. "Her bones are more reliable than the wind."

Korinna picked up the yellow linen again and punctured it with her needle, trying to stop the familiar fear from stitching itself around her heart.

What did a storm feel like in one's bones? For that matter, what would it feel like to experience the joy these women poured over each other like rain?

To feel anything except the fear?

A fierce rainstorm stopped the men from transporting Agathon's crates and barrels out to the ship. Agathon was furious at the delay, but none of the crew—including Tabitha's son—was willing to risk his life to ferry across the treacherous waves.

Tabitha was relieved that Matthias had tamed his impulses enough to refuse, but even with the storm, Agathon didn't release the men from his employ. They'd spent the day repacking goods in the warehouse, although Matthias had slipped away to share their midday meal.

She knew well the potential destruction at the hand of the sea, its power to splinter a boat, scattering the pieces into the water and wind. Isaac had died in such a storm, as if a leviathan had stirred up the water in its wrath, seeking vengeance until the sea swallowed his vessel. Her heart had splintered with the planks of the rowboat that he'd carefully constructed, the boat built to withstand any storm that had fallen under the crush of the waves.

Tonight the storm had calmed to a spattering of rain as Tabitha reclined on the cushions of the divan, tucked under the peristyle. Her bare feet stretched out from the shelter to indulge in the coolness, her reminder of God's grace. Ianthe's oils had helped ease some of her pain, but these dark hours gave her the most relief.

Closing her eyes, she listened to the patter of rain in the birdbath.

Almost twenty years ago, Agathon had lured Isaac away from her. Not with a woman but with the promise of more money. It had been a risk to fix one of the *Chiron's* masts in that storm. She and Isaac hadn't needed the income anymore—they'd saved plenty from Isaac's previous work—but Agathon had wanted to take the ship on a maiden voyage down the coast before he began shipping the wares he'd accumulated. He offered Isaac a substantial amount of money to work through a storm that lasted a week, preparing for this journey. Tabitha had begged her husband to wait, but Isaac wanted to finish this job well.

After completing the work, he and his small crew rowed back toward home.

And they'd almost made it.

The boat hit a rock, and while the other members were able to swim to shore, Isaac never came home. Agathon took charge after they found his body, helping her secure the grave over Joppa, but he'd refused to honor his commitment to pay her the full amount he'd offered Isaac.

She pulled her feet back out of the rain, tucking them under her skirt again.

Agathon never gave her the money, but the magistrate in Joppa wasn't fond of the sea merchant. He ruled that Agathon must give her, as Isaac's widow, thirty percent of any income made from the imports and exports of the *Chiron*, for as long as her husband's ship stayed afloat. Agathon cheated her out of most of this income, but she received enough to provide for her household and the church community that gathered here. The rest she invested into supplies for the widows who sewed with her.

Over the years, the return on her investments had somehow multiplied, like the stories of Jesus with the loaves and fishes. These women had plenty to sustain them, and she had plenty as well. Even though Agathon wasn't an honest man, Isaac had built a sturdy ship that continued providing for his household. And Agathon had despised her ever since, even after she became friends with his wife, for taking a significant portion of his income.

She opened her eyes and took a sip of the rosewater that Glykera had brought her, sweetened with honey.

Losing Isaac had been the worst season of her life. The second was losing her son.

Looking back, she'd almost wondered if Bethany's rejection somehow reminded him of the rejection from the woman who'd birthed him. Had he felt abandoned all over again? It seemed like everything he'd bunched up inside him for almost two decades spilled out in that one moment, in front of their entire church.

Somehow Joshua and Bethany recovered their marriage, but the community struggled to revitalize itself in the wake of Simon's frustration and the dissension among them. And the tension had sparked again now that Matthias had returned.

More than anything, she wanted Matthias to experience the redemption that she'd experienced long ago when she had decided to follow Christ. And she wanted him to find a wife who loved God and saw in him what she saw—a man with fire in his heart for those he loved. Someone who would fight for his family.

Had another woman captured his heart while he traveled? She didn't dare ask, but she'd worried that after falling so hard for Bethany, Matthias would never dare to give his heart away again. She'd wanted him to let go of his anger at the rejection and love again—someone other than Bethany.

Neither Joshua nor Bethany had returned to the community this week, but she'd seen how Matthias still looked at Bethany when he first came home. While he might be curious about Korinna, he hadn't lost his desire for his first love.

Matthias stepped into the courtyard, scanning the perimeter before he moved toward her. She patted the seat, and he accepted her offer, leaning his head back against the stone wall of the house, his right hand curled over the left to hide his missing thumb.

In the fading light, she could see the strength of his jawline, glad he had shaved the bristly whiskers off his face. His strength ran deep through his veins and served him well when it was channeled the right direction, sailing toward good instead of evil.

"Why are you sitting in the dark?" he asked.

"I lost track of the hour."

A comfortable silence rested between them, and she savored it before he spoke again. "Thank you for welcoming me back."

"You're always welcome here," she said, her heart quaking again at the thought of him going back to sea. "We missed you at dinner."

"I was trying to visit a friend."

Perhaps that was the reason Matthias had stayed here for the week. Perhaps it was the reason he'd finally returned home at all. It was much too late for him to have Bethany now, but she feared he was still focused—obsessed—on winning her.

"I'm worried for you, Matthias."

He glanced at her with a smile. "You worry too much."

She might not have birthed this man, but often it felt like he was just as stubborn as she. For all the good in him, for all the challenges he'd overcome with his confidence and tenacity, she wished that he could stop himself when the stakes were too high.

She leaned back against the cushion, the weariness returning to her heart and mind. And she prayed quietly for wisdom in how to soften the passion in his heart.

"Joshua will never divorce Bethany, if that's what you're wanting. He loves his wife."

"He's not supposed to be with her—"

"Nor is he supposed to divorce."

"Then perhaps we'll steal quietly away," he said.

Her head spun at the thought, the utter destruction it would bring to their entire community, but only the Messiah could stop him from hurting himself and those around him.

"Jesus wants to give freedom to each one of us," she said, desperately wanting him to understand. "He even called one of His best friends out of the grave, breaking him free from its chains."

He groaned. "I've already heard that story."

"No other God has conquered death, nor has one shown so much love to His children."

He squirmed on his seat like he'd done when he was a child.

"I'm praying that the Lord will change your mind, Matthias. That He will set you free of this."

He shook his head. "Prayer doesn't work, at least not for me."

She'd guessed that he had stopped believing, but it was the one thing, the one hope, that she had for him. No matter where he was or whom he married, she wanted him to know the peace and truth of the Savior.

"You must stop pursuing Bethany, before you hurt yourself and her."

"I haven't done anything—"

"But I fear that you will."

Perhaps it would be better for her son to return to Greece, at least until he stopped chasing after the wind that blew any direction it pleased. In the pagan world, maybe, he would realize his need to cling to a real God instead of a woman he couldn't have. That nothing in this life would heal the gaping wound inside.

Closing her eyes again, she prayed he would learn to be content in exactly who God made him to be. That he would find true peace, the kind that would gently mend his heart and direct him toward the course that God intended him to sail.

# CHAPTER TWELVE

The *Chiron's* hull was crammed with expensive fruits and fabrics and prized cedar from Lebanon. Most of the crew were spending the night on board so they could leave at first light, but Agathon wanted to recheck the warehouse before they sailed, so Matthias volunteered to row his employer to shore.

The past two evenings he'd spent pacing in front of Bethany's home, hoping she would emerge while Joshua was out fishing. He'd already promised Agathon that he would sail with him back to Greece, but he wanted Bethany to know that he would return within two months. He wouldn't abandon her.

In the midst of Agathon's frenzy—checking his locks and ledgers—Matthias snuck out to visit Bethany's house one last time. Agathon didn't care where Matthias slept, as long as he was ready to row back out at daybreak.

He'd already kissed his mother and Glykera goodbye, promising them both that he would return when Agathon sailed back to Joppa, but it was his decision to choose what he wanted to do with his future. He didn't know the names of his parents, but Greek blood ran through him, calling him back to Athens. There he could get whatever he wanted—food, women, drink. Waiting was a curse for those who didn't have the courage to pursue their dreams, and he wouldn't wait any longer here.

Somehow he would speak to Bethany before he left for Greece. Perhaps he could even convince her to leave with him. No one in Greece would care whether or not she'd been married in a distant place called Joppa.

Several lamps burned in this evening hour outside Simon's villa. Matthias jostled the front door, but it was latched. When the watchdog inside began barking, he backed away.

Matthias searched the upper windows, and his breath caught as if it were snatched up in a net and stolen away. He stepped closer again, a ship struggling to find land for the night, craving this light in the depths of his soul.

Bethany was perfectly framed inside the window, slowly brushing her long tresses, her face turned toward the stars. And he stood entranced for a moment, in awe of her beauty.

She deserved so much better than a fisherman who'd already lived half his life. She needed someone young who would fight for her. A man who wanted a partnership—in business and in a family with children they could rear together as husband and wife.

Joshua had stolen the greatest of treasures from Matthias. He was only retrieving what belonged to him. Nothing his mother or anyone else said would deter him.

After Joshua obtained a divorce, he and Bethany could return to Joppa. They'd finally put right this terrible wrong.

A fig tree grew underneath Bethany's chamber. Perhaps he could climb up, and they could escape down the stairs together. Her command would stop the watchdog's threat.

Lantern light spilled over him as he moved up to the tree, but its branches didn't climb far enough for him to scale. Perhaps she could tie off a bed linen and throw it down.

"Bethany," he called quietly.

He couldn't see her face, but at his words, she stepped away from the open window. Perhaps she was retrieving a linen or, better yet, hurrying down the steps to unlatch the front door. They wouldn't wait for two months. This very night, they'd escape together. As long as he promised Agathon his wage for the journey, the man would allow her to travel on the *Chiron*.

This very night Bethany would be with him.

His heart raced at the thought. Finally she would be his, and he would treasure her for a lifetime.

A quarter of an hour passed as he waited. The light still flowed in her room, but she didn't reappear at the window.

Was she still gathering her things for a journey? Perhaps she hadn't heard him after all.

He couldn't speak any louder for fear of Simon hearing him. While he'd be able to defend himself against this man, he couldn't fight their neighbors or the magistrate.

Something rustled down the lane, someone moving toward him, and his heart shivered within him.

But they were heavy steps traveling his way, not the light footfalls of a woman.

He ducked into the shadows, between two houses, waiting for the man to pass. But the man stopped at the front door and rang the bell.

Fire raged inside Matthias as he stepped out of the shadows. Joshua had returned home.

Matthias's fists balled, arms shaking as he rushed toward this thief of a man. But before he could reach Joshua, someone lifted the latch and Joshua stole through the front door.

Moments later, Bethany's quiet laughter filtered down to the cobblestone, and Matthias cringed at this sound. Was she pleased to see her husband? Surely not. She was only resigned to her fate. Perhaps she was trying to distract the man she'd been forced to marry. A little longer, and she'd join him on the street.

Soon, though, her lamp was extinguished, the curtains drawn, and in the stillness of the night, he heard Joshua's voice. Then Bethany spoke in return, telling this man she loved him. Words meant for Matthias.

Had she been mocking him all along? Watching him from the window tonight even as she waited for her husband? Speaking loud enough now on purpose for Matthias to hear? Every syllable nailed through his heart, every word rejected him again and again.

Matthias felt himself shrink inside. Back to the boy who'd been mocked for not being like the other children. The only boy who'd lost a mother and a thumb.

The boy who'd been left behind.

What had Joshua said to turn Bethany against him?

He stepped closer, his gaze still on the dark curtains. Then he raced toward the market. The stalls were packed up for the week, but the black stones that food merchants had used to build fire rings remained. He picked up the heaviest stone he could find, ash staining his hands, and rushed back to Simon's house.

He stood in the street again, every muscle inside him trembling. Then he lifted the stone over his head and heaved it upward. The rock sliced through the barrier of curtain, crashing into Bethany's room.

Someone cried out, but Matthias was already racing back through the maze of streets.

He'd prove to Bethany that she had made a mistake.

One day she would love him again.

"Open up!" A man shouted, pounding on Tabitha's front door.

She hopped off her bed in the upper room and crossed to the ledge. While she couldn't see who was knocking, he was certainly in earnest.

Her heart rolled as her mind slowly wakened. The *Chiron* was supposed to sail this morning. Had something happened to Matthias?

She'd sent him off yesterday with an extravagant meal that included Zoe and David and several men who'd been classmates in school. And she'd waved to him from the harbor as he, along with several of the crewmen, rowed for the final time out to the ship.

The man below shouted again, and Niles glanced around the edge of the makeshift wall that separated this upper room. "I'll find out who it is."

"Thank you." Tabitha quickly washed her face and tied back her hair, praying for peace to stop this panic that bled through her. No matter what happened now, she had to be calm.

She trailed Niles down the steps, waiting back in the shadows of the vestibule while he unlocked the door. The light from a lantern flooded inside.

"I must speak with Tabitha."

"Agathon?" She stepped quickly forward, wondering if he had news or if he was once again trying to torment her. "Why are you pounding on my door?"

The man stepped inside, his lantern blinding her as he held it up to her face. "Where is Matthias?"

Relief rushed through her with the question. If he was asking about Matthias, he knew of no accident.

The oil lantern swung in his hands, teetering light back and forth across the vestibule. "What happened to him?"

"Quiet your voice," she said.

"I will do no such thing."

"You will waken my neighbors—"

"I don't care who I waken."

Several dogs barked nearby. "I would be glad to check Matthias's room but only if you stop shouting."

She couldn't see his eyes in the blinding light, but he lowered his voice when he spoke again. "Hurry," he commanded. "We're supposed to leave at daybreak."

Shadows played across the fresco paintings as she walked back to the stairs. Instead of utilizing the upper room like the others in their household, Matthias had chosen to sleep in his former chamber on the second floor, as if he felt more secure within the stone walls than on the roof.

If there'd been an accident, Agathon would have known about it. Other boatmen would have seen it—or they'd be missing too.

The door into Matthias's room was open, and as she suspected, his bed was empty. If he wasn't on the ship—where had he gone?

Her bare feet felt heavy as she plodded back down to the vestibule, as if she had a chain wrapped around each ankle. Agathon was pacing in front of the open door, Niles standing in the shadows. Not that the older man could protect her from Agathon's wrath, but she was glad for the company.

Agathon lifted the lantern again. "Well?"

"He's not in his room."

"Where did he go?" Agathon's voice rose again, and she had nothing left to bargain for his silence.

"The last I saw him, he was paddling out to your ship."

"Well, he paddled me back in this evening," he said. "Then he disappeared."

"I don't know—"

"If he doesn't return within the hour, I'm going to leave Joppa without him!"

Matthias had talked of coming home one day, helping her with the business, but right now he seemed to be driven solely by what he couldn't have.

She sighed. "I suspect that's exactly what he wants."

Agathon leaned toward her, his purple-ringed nose bulging like a plum. "What is wrong with your son?"

Tabitha didn't respond. Just because Matthias didn't want to sail with Agathon didn't mean anything was wrong with him. But he did have a problem. Matthias loved deeper than most, his heart's desires overtaking those of his mind.

Agathon turned away, the lantern light splitting her street in two.

What did Matthias have planned? Or had he made a plan at all? Perhaps he would change his mind and meet Agathon at the harbor before the man hired someone else to row him out.

Niles returned to bed without a word, and after latching the door, she trekked back up the steps. Sleep wouldn't return so she leaned against the low wall and watched the sun rise above the hill.

Just as Agathon predicted, the *Chiron* disappeared with the coming of light, its wooden tunic fading as it moved into the distance. A square of material. A thread. A speck of dirt before the ocean washed it away.

"Oh, Matthias."

She whispered the words to no one but herself, but God knew the plea of her heart.

Had her son gone with Agathon or had he stayed?

If he'd stayed to pursue Bethany—only pain would follow his refusal to let go.

# CHAPTER THIRTEEN

Matthias sank amid the rocks on the shoreline, his heart pounding in this early-morning light. Ahead was the rock where the legendary Andromeda had been chained, a sacrifice to appease an angry monster.

A spray of seawater hit the stone wall, washing over him as if it could drown the anguish inside. He shouted into the spray, his anger mixing with the salt. Had he hurt Bethany? The rock wasn't meant for her, but in his fury...

He feared returning home, afraid of what he might find. He'd wanted to help Bethany, not hurt her, but he felt like the sea monster instead of the savior. Why did he bring ruin—pain—to those he loved? He had never meant to harm her. Not at the wedding feast or last night. He wanted to take care of her.

His mind swirled with the bits that he'd seen through her window, spinning inside him like they were trapped in a whirl-pool. How was he supposed to know the truth if he couldn't talk to Bethany? She was the only one who could tell him whether or not her love for him had changed.

For three days he wandered along sand dunes and the rocky shoreline, sleeping on the beach and stopping in villages to buy mediocre food. On Friday he returned to Joppa and visited the public bathhouse, washing and shaving before he went home. The community would think he'd left on the *Chiron*, and he hoped to find Bethany at their house church. If she was well, he'd praise all the gods, then he'd ask why she'd been mocking him from her window.

He washed his feet at the door, planning to head straight to the courtyard, but Glykera intervened when he walked back into the villa, waving him into the kitchen. He protested, wanting to see first if Bethany was well, but Glykera was relentless.

"You're supposed to be on the ship," Glykera said as she layered flatbread on a platter beside chunks of sheep's milk cheese.

"I decided not to leave after all."

"It would have been nice of you to inform your mother. She's been worried sick."

"I didn't mean to worry her," he said.

Glykera lifted a clay bowl off the shelf—a *mortarium*—and handed it to him along with a pestle. Then she dumped a handful of garlic into the bowl. "Crush these."

He placed the dish on the counter beside the *authepsa*, a bronze urn with coals at the bottom to heat water. "How is Bethany?"

She ignored his question. "Didn't they teach you how to cook on that ship?"

"They taught me plenty."

"Then do something useful and help me prepare the meal for your mother and all of those who've gathered in your home." She reached for the mortarium again and set it in front of him. "You have to grow up, Matthias. You no longer have the excuse of being only a boy."

He cringed at her words. Did she think he hadn't grown up? He'd tried to be mature, ask for Bethany's hand in marriage. "I haven't done anything wrong."

Glykera scrutinized him. "You've done plenty wrong, but you're too hardheaded to see it. Just like Agathon…"

He ground the pestle into the garlic. "I am nothing like that man."

She swept back a stray piece of her gray hair. "You're not as smart as you think, Matthias."

"I never said that I was smart."

"But you think it. Just like Agathon. Anger is not the same as wisdom. A fool thinks he is the smartest man of them all. A wise person may stumble, but he makes amends for any harm he's caused."

Matthias pointed the pestle at her. "I believe you just called me a fool."

"Only God knows a man's heart and mind."

"God doesn't seem to care about my heart or my mind. He might love Imma, but if there is a God above all gods, He seems to hate me…."

Glykera studied him for a moment. "On one hand you think far too highly of yourself, Matthias, and on the other, you don't realize the strength that you have, the ability to love well. God does love you, and you'd know it if you'd only focus on what you have instead of what you think you're missing."

He ground the pestle again, pressing his frustration into the garlic. He could argue with Glykera, but besides Imma, this woman knew him better than almost anyone. She might even know him better than his own mother, because while Imma focused on the good in him, Glykera saw both the good and bad and still loved him.

Glykera placed her hand on his shoulder. "You can stop now."

He glanced down at the shreds of garlic puddled on the clay. Somehow he'd lost himself in his work.

Glykera dumped the garlic into a separate bowl of oil and mixed it. "You are not going out into that room if you're going to cause some sort of disturbance. Your mother's heart will fail her."

"I'm not going to disturb anyone."

"Take this outside." She shoved the bowl of garlic and oil at him. "You're a man now, Matthias. It's time for you to take care of her instead of the other way around."

He snatched a few pieces of bread on his way out, then handed the bowl of garlic off to someone he didn't know so they could deliver it to the table. Hiding himself behind the fig tree, he searched for Bethany from the back of the courtyard. She was there, eating with her family near the front, and relief washed through him. He hadn't wounded her with the stone, but Joshua had a swollen eye.

Perhaps he should have thrown the rock harder.

When the meal ended, Bethany stepped up to play her lyre. Now she saw him, and those beautiful brown eyes, the ones that had haunted his dreams, watched him closely as she sang, almost as if she were inviting him forward.

Or was she mocking him like she'd done from the window?

He shook his head in an attempt to sort out the confusion inside. Bethany hadn't been mocking him. The way she looked at him now, she must still care for him.

No one else noticed his presence until Simon stood to read through another letter from the man named Peter, an apostle visiting the nearby town of Lydda. Simon glared a warning at him before lifting the papyrus.

Matthias didn't hear what he said, his gaze refocused on Bethany's shoulders. What would those around him do if he pushed through this small crowd and demanded to speak with her now?

His mother turned as if sensing the scene that played out in his mind. Then she left her place beside Korinna and shuffled back to the tree.

"What are you doing here?" she whispered.

He nodded toward the front. "I want to speak with Bethany."

"You have to be able to talk to me as well," she said. "This coming and going without telling me where you are—"

"I've been wandering up the coast, thinking," he said. "I've decided that I want to come home again for a season. If you'll have me."

Imma glanced up at Bethany. "Until she changes her mind?"

"Perhaps," he said, his gaze fixed on her again.

"But what if she wants to stay with Joshua?"

A curse slipped through his lips, his answer to the absurdity of this question. Several people looked their way, but Simon continued reading, ignoring the interruption.

Imma's voice shook when she spoke again. "You are going to get yourself—get both of us—in trouble, Matthias. And Bethany—"

"Doesn't your God tell you not to fear?"

She was quiet for a moment, seeming to process his question. "You are right, Son, but I am still afraid, mostly for you."

He reached for her hand. "You don't need to fear for my sake."

His mother stood quietly beside him, gripping his hand as Simon finished the letter.

"'I urge each of you to continue living in peace.'" Simon read the apostle's words. "'I have known strife, and to my great regret, I have caused strife. I ask that you resolve any difference between you quietly, with prayer and grace, and love each other as Christ Jesus our Lord loves you. Pluck out the weeds before they threaten the harvest in your heart.'"

The words caught Matthias even as he tried to deflect the message. This Peter didn't know him, didn't know what happened here.

He glanced around the room, wondering if everyone was staring back at him, but they seemed to be engrossed by this letter. Then he realized Simon had probably written this apostle and told him exactly what happened in their community. Had he mentioned Matthias by name?

"'Our God, who can breathe life back into those He loves, who can resurrect both bodies and minds, wants you to be healthy in both heart and soul,'" Simon continued, "'and I want the church in Joppa to yield a bountiful harvest of fruit. *Pax tecum.*'"

*May peace be with you.*

Simon probably didn't tell Peter how he'd wronged someone in the church. How his daughter had loved Matthias and that the man robbed them both of their marriage.

Simon had thought he'd ruined Matthias, but the man had only strengthened him. If this God could really perform miracles, then He would do a miracle for Matthias and give him Bethany as a bride. If He could raise people from the dead, He could surely take life as well. Joshua was a man who deserved to die for stealing Bethany.

When the service ended, Simon and his family slipped again out the back.

Imma took his hand, tears streaming down her face. "I want you to stay, Matthias. I want you to come to church here and partner with me and the Rhapsodies to sell our wares in the market, but you have to stop pursuing her."

"I can't—"

"If not," she said sadly, "you'll have to find someplace else to live."

# CHAPTER FOURTEEN

It's almost done." Tabitha held up Korinna's wedding garment, the sunlight capturing the lilac color as if it were one
of her garden flowers.

Korinna touched the sleeve before recoiling her hand.
"Which means Agathon will be home soon."

The man had been gone for more than a month now.
Before he left, Tabitha had sent a written invitation for him
to attend their gathering, but she'd received no reply. After
he married Korinna, she doubted Agathon would allow her
friend to continue attending the Rhapsodies or their church
community. The completion of this garment signaled the
end of her time with this young woman whom she'd grown to
love.

"We still need to embroider the sleeves," Tabitha said,
reminding them both that they still had a little time left. A few
weeks perhaps.

"Can you teach me to embroider?"

"Of course," she said. "And I expect you will learn just as
quickly as you've learned how to sew."

After a delayed start, Korinna had poured herself into this
garment as if it could cover up the sorrow in her heart. Her
husband might not appreciate it, but he would have a beautiful

bride on their wedding day, dressed in a lovely robe made with her own hands.

Pain raced through Tabitha's head, and she rubbed her temples. The headaches came more frequently now, and some days the anchors on her legs weighed even heavier. But as long as God kept bringing people to her to love, she wouldn't stop serving.

Korinna studied her. "Is your head hurting again?"

Tabitha lowered her hands, not wanting to alarm Korinna when she had enough cares of her own. "It usually leaves as quickly as it comes."

"I will ask Glykera to make you some tea," Korinna said.

Tabitha smiled, grateful for her concern. "She's already heating water."

"Perhaps Matthias can buy some clove oil in Jerusalem."

She nodded. Matthias had seemed to make good on his promise in the past month to avoid Bethany. While it pained her to see him skipping the church services, he had poured himself into their business, which included working each Tuesday at their market stall, selling more in a month than she'd sold last year.

All the Rhapsodies were ecstatic at the surge in their income since Matthias took over and were quite relieved that they no longer had to peddle their own wares. They sewed even faster on their mornings together so they could increase their inventory. Each hour of stitching was another *qab* of flour to make bread, an extra coin or two to purchase a pomegranate or cluster of grapes for their families.

The women always stitched with hope, but Matthias's skills were turning the seeds of their dreams into a thriving garden. And, in the process, he was earning a small percentage of each sale. The profits, she prayed, would grow rapidly for all of them so he could continue selling these goods.

After the market today, he would to travel down to Jerusalem and then to Galilee to obtain more linen so he could begin selling their finely stitched garments beyond the province of Judea.

Another pain pierced her head. Ianthe's oil had helped, but it was almost gone and she'd been too tired to search for her friend. Next time she saw Ianthe, she'd ask to purchase more. The woman may not be able to sew, but Tabitha wondered if they could partner together in selling oils. That venture would provide much better than Ianthe's work as a scavenger.

She carefully folded Korinna's wedding garment and placed it in her basket before covering it with a lid. Soon Laurel, the servant who oversaw Agathon's home, would arrive to escort Korinna home. "I'm glad you were able to come an extra day this week."

"I told Laurel that Agathon would be furious if my tunic wasn't done in time for the wedding."

"Which is true—"

"And I wanted to talk with you while everyone was gone." Korinna glanced at the door. "Will Matthias return soon?"

She shook her head. "Not for hours."

Korinna watched a finch splashing in the bath, water soaking the lavender sprigs below them and flinging across to the rose bushes nearby.

Tabitha studied the woman's profile, the fixed eyes that had seen much in their sixteen years. They had much in common, Korinna and Matthias. They were so similar, both of them abandoned when they were young. Both trying to find their own way without a father to protect and guide them.

Both of them desperately needing the care and hope of a heavenly Father.

Korinna turned toward her. "I don't want to marry Agathon."

"I know," Tabitha said slowly. "I can't save you from this marriage, no matter how much I want to, but we can pray together that the Messiah will keep you from harm. More than rescuing you from this marriage, He wants to rescue your heart."

"I think—" Korinna rubbed her hands together, her gaze on the flowers. "I want to know your Savior, Tabitha, but…"

In spite of her hesitation, Tabitha's heart soared. This is what she wanted more than anything in this world, for those she loved to know the truth and experience the forgiveness that she'd known. While God might not free Korinna from marriage, He could give her freedom within it. Agathon, with all of his need for control, couldn't control Korinna's mind or her heart. And their Messiah would walk alongside her friend if she asked Him to join her.

"What is stopping you?" Tabitha asked.

"You call this God Master," she replied quietly. "And I must serve another lord."

"This Master, the Messiah, loves you more than you can ever imagine," Tabitha said, reaching for one of Korinna's hands.

"No one has ever loved me before, not like that. The gods have all been cruel—"

"God wants nothing but good for you, Korinna. His way isn't always easy, but He will help you serve Agathon in this life even as you ultimately serve Him."

"I want in Him what you have." Korinna scooted closer, both hands now embraced in Tabitha's. "I need Him, I think, more than anything."

"Yes," Tabitha said with a smile. "I believe you do."

"But I don't know how to follow—"

"You simply choose," Tabitha said. "You make a decision—a declaration—with your lips and then follow after the teachings of the Messiah with all of your heart."

Korinna slowly processed her words. "I'm ready."

Tabitha cradled their clutched hands to her heart and prayed with this young woman whom she'd come to love like a daughter, prayed that God, through His Son, would wash away every sin and embrace her with His love.

"I believe in You," Korinna prayed. "And I want to serve You with my life. Please forgive me for the things I've done wrong."

When they finished praying, a smile spread across Korinna's face, and the joy on her face was breathtaking, like one of the roses.

Tabitha gently squeezed her hands. "It won't be always easy, but our Lord will be beside you on the journey, no matter where it leads. He'll offer His hand to help you whenever you need it most."

"Korinna?" a woman called from the vestibule.

She dropped Tabitha's hands. "That's Laurel."

"Why don't you invite her to join us for the community meal tomorrow?"

"I always invite her, but she won't join us."

"It doesn't hurt to continue asking." Tabitha smiled at her again. "God loves her as much as He loves you and me."

"This stunning tunic with embroidered sleeves," Matthias called from the stall, "is a bargain at twenty denarii."

Two young women, accompanied by their mother, stopped and stared at the garment. Matthias draped the light fabric over the counter so they could imagine themselves wearing it to a wedding or, better yet, to one of their weddings.

"It's a piece of fine art." He smiled at them. "You'll be the envy of women across Israel."

The ladies huddled together before the oldest daughter looked back at him, returning his smile. The mother shuffled them away, but he suspected they would be back…and pay full price. Nothing in this market compared to the quality or artistry of the Rhapsodies' work. And few people from this area went to Jerusalem to shop for goods.

Imma was a natural saleswoman, bold in her determination to help each Rhapsody sell her wares. The men and women in Joppa shook their heads at her boldness, but they all respected her. Still, many of those who visited the market, prepared to make a purchase, wanted the approval of a man.

Matthias had learned how to bargain from his mother, but somehow, by doing the exact thing she would have done, he was able to sell the garments for much more. It was confounding that his presence elevated the value, but Imma was quite pleased with the results. Zoe and the others had begged him not to leave.

One day soon, Bethany would respect him again. While he honored his mother's request for now, he refused to lose sight of why he stayed in Joppa.

A man from the countryside walked toward him, a fisherman, perhaps. Matthias hung the fancy tunic on a peg and reached for a simpler day garment, the fabric a dove gray.

He leaned forward, waiting to display his wares so he didn't frighten this potential buyer. "Are you looking to purchase something for yourself?"

The man eyed Matthias warily. "I'm looking for something I can afford to buy for my wife."

Matthias carefully smoothed the garment as if it were worth a fortune and then laid it across the counter. "You have come to the right place to find quality at a reasonable price."

The man fingered the fabric as if he were a connoisseur, and then the two men began negotiating the sale back and forth, a fish and fisherman tugging on the invisible line before they settled at eight denarii. Enough for a reasonable profit for the Rhapsodies and a good purchase for this man. His wife would indeed be pleased.

Matthias slipped the coins into his pouch before he held up another garment, searching the crowd for someone who might be shopping for a new tunic. Or someone he might be able to convince of their need.

"The most beautiful tunic in all—" His words faded when he caught a glimpse of a familiar face in the crowd, at the brown curls escaping a cloth banded around her knot of hair.

Bethany was looking back at him. And she was alone.

Simon operated a stall down the lane, selling the leather that he'd tanned, but Matthias had managed to avoid him on these market days. He hung the tunic back on its peg and slipped out from behind the booth, quickly covering the short space between them. So many questions had haunted him, questions only she could answer. Finally, he could ask her directly about the past and their future.

"Hello, Bethany," he said, a school of villagers swimming around both sides of them.

In her hands was a heavy ceramic jar, an amphora of oil sloshing up to the rim. "I—I didn't know you were here."

"I've decided to stay in Joppa," he said, waiting for relief or anticipation to brighten her eyes. But instead of smiling, he saw a glimpse of fear.

She should be afraid of Joshua, not him.

"I help Imma at her booth every week. I thought everyone in the church knew—"

"We don't talk about you anymore, Matthias."

He leaned back against a stall. "But you did at one time...."

"Of course." She nodded toward the spice merchant she'd been speaking with moments before, indicating that she would return. Then she looked back at him. "It will be good for Tabitha to have you near."

"And perhaps good for us?"

She shook her head. "There is no *us*, Matthias."

"But there will be," he said, lowering his voice. "We just need a plan."

"My life has already been planned...."

He wished he could take her hand or, better yet, take her in his arms and keep her from harm.

"When you wounded my whole family, you wounded any relationship between us."

"Your family wounded me!" he insisted. "Simon wouldn't let us marry."

Bethany studied him closely, as if to judge whether or not he might try to sweep her away like he did last year.

"It's still not too late," he began. "We could..."

She waved one of her hands, stopping him. "My father wouldn't let us marry because I didn't want to marry you."

She didn't want to marry him?

He started to speak again, to retort her words, but he saw truth in the chestnut brown of her eyes. And it felt as if the entire hill might cave in on top of him. All his plans, his dreams, shattered in that moment, avalanching around him. All these years, he thought she loved him as much as he loved her. He'd thought he only needed to rescue her.

"You did want to marry me," he pressed, but the strength in his voice had drained away, seeming to dump out in the sea below them, drifting off to other parts of the world.

"I was interested in you a long time ago," she said. "Intrigued. But Joshua was the man that I loved with all my heart both then and now—and Joshua loves me."

"That's not true." He waved his hands in front of him as if he could scatter her words into the wind before they rooted inside him. Bartering them away.

"It is the truth." Her slender hands went to her scalp, as if she could still feel the pain of what happened a year ago.

"You loved me," he insisted. "I know it."

"That's the problem," she said. "You never seem to realize that you have a problem. That you might need to change. God loves you most soundly, but I never loved you as a wife should love her husband."

He gripped his fists together, wanting to shake her, to demand that she tell the truth, because this wasn't the truth. This was foolishness. Drivel.

What had Simon done to make her hate him when she had so clearly wanted to marry him last year? Simon and Joshua had poisoned her heart with their lies.

"I have to return home to my husband." Bethany swiveled on her heels, her back to him once again, but Matthias wasn't going to let her walk away.

He reached for her, trying to turn her back to him, but when he tugged her shoulders, the ceramic jar fell from her hands. She screamed when it splintered on her toes, oil splashing across the dirt lane and the hems of those nearby.

The crowd parted around them in a circle like waves rolling out from the toss of a stone. And then Simon was there, standing over his daughter before lifting her up in his arms. Blood covered her feet, dripping off her sandals, and Matthias felt something tear inside him as well.

"I'm sorry—"

"Leave me alone, Matthias." Bethany buried her head into the strength of her father's chest, her shoulders shuddering in what must be her silent cries.

Simon glared over at him. "She said to leave her alone."

He nodded once, resolute. "I will."

# CHAPTER FIFTEEN

**K**orinna watched the ceramic shatter at Bethany's feet, saw Simon pick up his daughter and clutch her to his chest. Then Matthias ran from the street like he was escaping from a den of lions, leaving behind a stall filled with the goods he was supposed to protect.

"Would you like anything else?" the merchant asked Korinna.

"No." She slipped her coin across the counter and stored the packet of salt in her pouch.

Bethany was sobbing on her father's shoulder, the blood from her feet dripping down his tunic. A crowd of people gathered around Simon, but no one followed after Matthias.

The man didn't understand how fortunate he was to have a mother like Tabitha. Instead he continued to throw away all that he had been given as if these gifts were nothing more than trash for the dump.

If only she could help calm the chaos inside him, the son of the woman she adored, before he broke Tabitha's heart for good.

As Matthias raced toward the harbor, she decided that even if Laurel yelled at her for tardiness, even if she sequestered Korinna to her chamber, the heavenly Master would want her to help Tabitha's son.

She rushed to his stall, swiftly unhooked the displayed garments, and folded each one into a stack, hiding them underneath the counter lest someone steal them. Then she followed Matthias's path to the shore.

She found him sitting on a bed of pebbles, as shattered as the jar he'd broken.

She slipped down beside him, the water lapping toward them but not yet touching their feet. He'd only spoken to her once before, when Tabitha introduced him, but she'd watched him over the past month. And she'd seen the sorrow in Tabitha's eyes. He might not like her words, but he needed to hear them.

"You can't keep running away, Matthias."

He wiped his sleeve across his face, his eyes focused on the gray horizon. "What do you know about running?"

Some slaves would have run by now, she supposed, instead of marrying their master, but she had no place to go. Perhaps it was cowardly, but she liked to think it was courage that kept her here. She knew what she faced and had accepted this fate.

"You should go to Athens," he said.

"You think I would escape abuse there?"

He wiped his face again. "I don't know."

"Injustice, I'm told, is everywhere."

He glanced back at the city. "It seems to be centered here in Joppa."

She tilted her head slightly as she studied him. He was handsome with his ebony hair trimmed close to his head, his face cleanly shaven, dark blue eyes that blazed with Grecian fire in the afternoon light. His hand passed out of his sleeve to wipe off his face one more time, and she stared at it. While his fingers were intact, his thumb was gone.

When he realized she was staring, he recoiled his arm and hid it again under his sleeve. Her eyes back on the ocean, she pretended she didn't see it.

"Were you born here?" he asked.

"I'm not certain."

She felt him looking at her now, but she didn't return his gaze. Nor did she want to talk about the little that she knew about her past.

"But how did Agathon—" He paused. "How did he obtain you for his service?"

"His wife bought me when I was about three. I don't remember where I lived before."

"Did Selene want to adopt you?" he asked.

Her past wasn't his business, yet she learned from Tabitha that sharing one's story could help others heal. "Perhaps." She pried a pebble from the folds of her skirt and tossed it back into the ocean. "Agathon never would have allowed it since he wanted a son. I worked in the kitchen as a child, but Selene always treated me with kindness. She called me her servant, never a slave."

"Agathon should have redeemed you after she died."

She pulled her legs to her chest, praying for boldness in her words. This man would respect nothing less. "No one except the Messiah can redeem me."

"It's a farce, this God that my mother purports. I love her, but no God can save us from death."

Tabitha needed her son, but even more Matthias needed to know, to understand, that He was deeply loved. "God can redeem you."

His eyes blazed again. "I don't need anyone to rescue me!"

"Slavery doesn't always mean that someone has bought you, Matthias. It seems to me that you've enslaved yourself."

He stared at her as if he were stunned by her boldness.

"I have no choice but to stay with Agathon, but you have a choice. You don't have to let the loss of Bethany imprison you."

"I haven't lost her!" he insisted. "I still love—"

"You think it's love to try to drag a woman off on her wedding day?"

His head coiled back as if she'd slapped him. "Simon treated me like garbage."

"I heard you punched his brother in the face," she said. "And then pulled out Bethany's hair."

The sea collided with a nearby cliff, misting their clothes. "She didn't deserve that," he said. "I should have pulled out Joshua's hair."

"Why did you try to kiss her?" she asked softly.

"I don't remember…." He folded over his lap, pressing his hands against the hem of his garment. "I don't remember much from that day except Bethany wouldn't leave with me."

"And so you ran—"

"I had no choice."

"But you have a choice now," she said. "A million choices."

"She was supposed to marry me. Simon and Joshua schemed against me, and I lost the fight."

She sighed. "A woman isn't a prize to be knocked down and dragged away. You have to slowly win her heart."

He shook his head as he sat tall again beside her. "I've never done anything slowly in my life."

She stood up. "Go home, Matthias, and start again."

He didn't say anything.

"Apologize to Simon and ask about Bethany's health."

"Simon will never speak to me again."

"Then perhaps you can write him a letter," she said. "You'll find a way."

He glanced up the northern shore as if he could see Caesarea from here.

"Starting today, you should run *to* something," she said, "not away."

# CHAPTER SIXTEEN

The frantic knocking reminded Tabitha of Agathon's visit a month ago, the night Matthias had gone missing. She hadn't expected the man to return for several more weeks. Perhaps he was anxious to proceed with his wedding plans.

That thought made her head pound even more.

Closing her eyes, Tabitha tried to block out the raging light in her bedroom chamber, but the rays slipped around the shutters that Niles had closed and seared through the crease of her eyelids. The room was sweltering and stank of onions and cabbage from the pack Glykera had applied to her forehead.

She had longed for cool before, but she'd never craved darkness with this much fervor. The night, Tabitha prayed, would bring relief to the throbbing and Glykera would return soon with a poultice made from anything except onions.

Someone pounded again, her brass knocker hammering against wood, and she hoped Niles would answer their caller soon before the sound mauled a hole through her head.

Ianthe, the Lord bless her, had brought another tincture. The medicine helped relieve some of the pain that festered in spite of the tea and various packs that Glykera applied, but this knocking was agony.

Matthias would return home soon—perhaps he would speak with their visitor about his or her concern and then come upstairs to tell her about his day at the market. No matter how much her head hurt, she always welcomed him and his stories.

"Tabitha?" It was Niles standing beside her bed, his voice soft. "Simon the Tanner is below and he insists upon seeing you."

"Can it wait until the morning?" she asked, pressing the onion pack with her palm. The aching should be gone by first light.

"He says that it cannot."

A tremor raced through her. Simon was a relatively calm man unless riled, and his knock had been charged by lightning.

"Has Matthias returned home from the market?" she asked.

"Not yet."

She feared he was the reason for Simon's anger.

Groaning, she sat up slowly on her bed. "Send him in."

Simon must have been waiting right outside her door because seconds later, he followed Niles into her room. "I'm sorry you're unwell, Tabitha, but I have some distressing news that we must discuss."

Every word nailed into her skull as she struggled to understand. "Could you please lower your voice?"

He reached for a chair and pulled it beside her bed, the stench of his garment, the smell of animal skins, overpowering the onions.

His next words were persistent but thankfully much quieter. "Matthias accosted my daughter at the market today."

Her heart plunged.

"She was trying to shop and he—" The man's voice crumbled. "Matthias has to stop antagonizing her."

She—and her son—knew this, yet Matthias couldn't seem to leave the woman alone. "Is Bethany injured?"

"She has broken several toes but, thank God, will recover. She'll need to remain at home for a season."

Her heart tore at the thought of Matthias wounding anyone, especially this woman who used her gifts so beautifully to glorify God. How had he broken her toes? While she wanted to know, she didn't dare ask.

Tabitha shifted on the pillow. "He doesn't intentionally hurt her."

"But he continues to do so. Until Bethany is better..." He glanced at the curtain over her window as if he could see the street below. "Until she is well again, the church will need to meet in my courtyard."

She reached for Ianthe's tincture, rubbing the essence of these flowers into her temples again. "We can't accommodate the entire community in that space."

"I know," he said, struggling to keep his voice low. "I thought you and Matthias and the women in your group could continue worshipping here. You could easily lead them, Tabitha."

And then she understood. Simon wasn't accommodating his daughter during her recovery as much as he was splitting their group into two.

She'd heard of other followers who'd divided over how to best follow their Messiah, but she'd never dreamed it might happen here in Joppa. Until now, they had cared for each other like family—promoting the good and swiftly resolving their differences. She couldn't blame Simon for not wanting to worship with Matthias, but a division—this loss spurred by her son—still cut to the core.

She wanted to reach out in her pain, beg this elder to remain united, but he wouldn't rescind after what Matthias had done. "We have to forgive him, Simon."

"But even in forgiveness, he can't be near Bethany. If he speaks to her again, we'll have to ask the magistrate to intervene."

This community was her backbone. Her family. God had used them to give her the strength to lead the Rhapsodies and serve in ways that she'd never dreamed. How could she continue without them by her side?

She looked back at the man, trying to focus her eyes. "What happens when Matthias leaves Joppa?"

"Bethany should be well enough to return to your courtyard."

But what if Matthias didn't leave? If he decided to continue his work here at her side, what she wanted more than anything in this life. She would have to choose between her son and her church. The division within their community, she feared, would never mend.

Simon was right to protect his family, but in that moment, she felt as if she was being abandoned by those who were supposed to love her most.

Light sailed around the curtain again, another sharp pain ricocheting through her. "I understand," she finally said. "You have to do what is the best for everyone."

"We love you as a dear sister, Tabitha, but until Matthias stops pursuing Bethany and decides to become a brother to her and the other women in the church…"

She stopped him. "The Rhapsodies and I and Matthias will meet here for now."

"It's only for a season, Tabitha."

But these types of seasons, she knew well, could last for a lifetime.

The bliss of sleep comforted Tabitha like a woolen blanket on the coldest of days. A respite in a sea of pain. When she woke again, it was still dark outside, but she could hear the eve of morning in the rooster's crow.

Soon the sunlight would return, and her headache, perhaps, with it. But for now, the pain had been pressed into a dull ache, her thoughts bubbling back up in her head like new wine.

She hadn't visited Isaac's grave in weeks, and now it was as if Elohim Himself was calling her from the depths of her heart, asking her to climb back up the hill above Joppa and visit the grave before the Rhapsodies arrived. Perhaps He wanted to prepare her heart and mind this morning before she told these sisters about the changes in their church.

She dressed quickly and descended the stairs to the second floor, the sound of Matthias's breath trickling out into the hallway. He'd returned home last night, and for that she was glad, but she wasn't prepared yet at this hour to speak with him.

As the first warmth of morning trickled through the kitchen window, Tabitha drank a cup of tepid water and wrapped a piece of flatbread and several chunks of cheese in a cloth to fuel her walk. Then she bundled together stems of hyacinths and rushed out the front door before Glykera could find her and insist that she return to bed with a pack of onions and cup of tea steeped with ground cinnamon and valerian root.

Her steps were much slower than they'd been on her climb the last time, the anchors around each leg sinking deeper into the dirt path, but she didn't stop moving as the sun crept over the horizon, her heart calling her to pray in the grove in whatever way that God led.

The soft rays of light didn't blind her like she'd feared. Instead they seemed to beckon her on. She pushed herself forward in spite of the weight threatening to topple her back down into Joppa.

At the top of the hill, she turned right toward the dump, her gaze on the green ribbon of trees beyond the trash. At the place where the Spirit of God felt most real to her, as if she could breathe in His presence after she passed this stench of rubbish.

A rooster crowed near the trash, far later than the others that crowed in the city. As the sound petered out, Tabitha turned from the olive grove, scanning the garbage pile that had grown significantly in both height and breadth since she'd found Matthias all those years ago. Her mind journeyed back in time for a moment to that long season of grief after her husband died. To the finding of a boy whom God used to change everything in her life.

The rooster crowed again—no, it wasn't a rooster.

She listened carefully, her heart pounding. It was a cry, a baby's cry, coming from the dump.

Tabitha forgot the aching in her head, the call of her heart to pray. She dropped the flowers and scrambled over the mound. As if she could rescue Matthias all over again.

She rummaged through the pile like the women who searched for treasure, searched until she found a baby girl abandoned to exposure, not even a blanket to protect her from the wind or sun.

No one else was out yet searching for something valuable hidden in the garbage. It was only her and this baby and the threat of sunlight that had already burnt her skin.

The child was whimpering, her cry much weaker now than Matthias's had been. Tabitha marveled that she survived the night alone, if she'd been here all night. She was only a few weeks old and wouldn't survive much longer if nothing was done for her.

God, it seemed, hadn't called her up the hill to pray after all. He'd called her to rescue another child.

How could she ever doubt that He still spoke to her? His voice was quiet but strong, a gentle but fervent prodding from deep within when she needed to move.

And right now, she needed to hurry.

The pain in her head gained strength with the warmth of the sun, and she knew that she must hurry for this girl's sake. Tabitha reached down and tore the seam of her tunic, but she couldn't rip the weave of cloth. With the baby secure in one arm, she searched the edge of the trash until she found a rusted tool.

The baby began crying again when Tabitha placed her on the ground, but she needed both hands, one holding out the linen and the other to clench the tool.

Carefully she tore two lengths of material from her gown, the meticulously stitched tunic unraveling into several pieces near the bottom. One of the pieces she used to clean off the coating of soil and dust from the baby's skin. The other she wrapped carefully around the girl's body before lifting her again.

Her feet felt light again, if only for a moment, as she hurried back toward Joppa, praying now that the pain in her head wouldn't paralyze her before she arrived at the doctor's home. And that this baby, who'd grown quiet again, wouldn't die on the walk down the hill.

But as she drew closer to the city, her arms and legs grew heavy again, her breath labored, and she feared she might collapse, the baby perishing alongside her.

Surely God didn't send her all this way for them both to die. He wouldn't abandon them now.

Her vision blurred, the sea spilling onto the land below, but on the path, she saw someone climbing up the hill. Someone, she supposed, coming to forage in the dump. Perhaps if she paid this person, he or she would help her escort this baby to the physician.

It was a woman on the trail, her gaze focused on the ground, but Tabitha recognized the olive-colored tunic. In that moment, she praised God for His gracious answer to her prayer.

"Ianthe!" she called.

The woman glanced up, and when she saw Tabitha, she rushed up the path.

As Ianthe drew near, Tabitha held out her arms, the baby resting between them. "Could you please take her?"

Ianthe looked down at the child in shock. Instead of reaching out, her arms pressed firmly against her sides.

"Please," Tabitha begged. "We need to get her to a doctor right away, and my body is failing me."

The dust and rocks, the blues of the sea, swirled around her. Any moment, she would…

Ianthe thrust out her arms and took the girl. While the woman still didn't speak, she changed her course quickly to escort Tabitha back down to Joppa.

Tabitha blinked, her world clearing with the strength of this friend.

"I found her at the dump," she said quietly. "Someone left her."

Ianthe muttered something in return, and Tabitha leaned toward her. "I'm sorry. I didn't hear—"

This time Ianthe spoke louder. "It's not important."

"All words are important."

But the words were lost between them as Ianthe began singing to the baby girl. Even though Tabitha no longer carried the weight of a child, she lagged behind her older friend, her head throbbing again as if it had given her a respite only to rescue this child.

She collapsed onto one of the many rocks that salted the countryside. "Please take her to Abel, the physician. I will follow soon."

Ianthe glanced down at the baby, then back at Tabitha. "I'm not leaving either of you alone."

Tabitha closed her eyes, trying to block out the light. When she opened them again, the swimming in her mind stilled long enough to see the azure splash of sea. And something in the distance.

She squinted at the horizon, and Ianthe's gaze swept across the Mediterranean with her until she confirmed what Tabitha saw—sails like white blossoms clinging to the branches of a ship. Another boat might be visiting Joppa, but she suspected those sails belonged to the *Chiron*.

Agathon's ship in their harbor. Her son's choices that divided her church family. The baby girl who'd stopped stirring in Ianthe's arms.

The relentless pain inside her head pounded even harder as she tried to process it all.

She needed to do something to bring their community together again, but everything, it seemed, was collapsing around her.

# CHAPTER SEVENTEEN

The basin turned red when Matthias lowered his foot into the water. He'd bandaged the skin last night with a scrap piece of his mother's fabric, but the shreds of old linen were now soaked with blood and the wound had broken open again.

After what happened, he'd wanted to run far away, but he was hardly able to walk by the time he'd arrived at the shore. He'd cursed the skies for his foolishness. For Bethany's denial. For the injury that kept him from running to Caesarea or beyond.

When Korinna sat down beside him on the gravel, he'd hidden his feet. She had already seen the humiliating display in the market—he didn't want her to see the cuts on his skin as well. Bethany was the one they should worry about anyway. The woven straps of her sandals would have offered no protection against the jagged shards, the heavy pounding of oil, on her feet. The injury that, once again, he'd caused.

He wished he could check on Bethany, tell her that he was sorry, but if Simon hadn't called for the magistrate yet, he would surely do so if Matthias showed up at his home.

Glykera would question the bloody linen wrapped around his foot and so would his mother. If Imma didn't know yet what he'd done to Bethany, she would find out soon enough. And when she did, he would assure her that he was embarking back on the *Chiron* when it returned to port. Not to run away this time but to protect all of them. Imma loved him, that he was certain of, but he could no longer trust himself.

He'd thought Simon had wronged him by withholding Bethany from a marriage, but if Bethany was telling him the truth, she'd never wanted to marry him. All along he'd thought she loved him, but he had believed a lie. The thought hurt much worse than the pain in his foot. It cut right through skin and bone, shattering his heart.

Things had been going well for him in the past month. He'd enjoyed his work at the market, the triumph of a sale, much more than he'd ever enjoyed sailing for Agathon. But, once again, he'd wrecked what he had wanted to build, crushed the hope within him, and hurt the people he loved. Whenever something good was about to happen, he sabotaged it. While he desperately wanted to stop ruining things for himself, stop hurting his mother, something within him warred against what he wanted to do.

Voices rang out below. The Rhapsodies were gathering this morning and in several hours, the church community would arrive. His injured foot would prevent him from beginning his journey to Caesarea today, but he wouldn't go downstairs to join the community either, no matter what Imma asked of him. None of them would want him there anyway, and he couldn't bear to see Bethany, the disdain in her eyes or the anger from Simon and Joshua.

In the midst of the voices, he heard a baby's cry, and he straightened in his chair. None of the Rhapsodies, to his knowledge, had a baby. Had his mother invited someone else into their home?

With all that was happening, she had to stop opening their door to anyone who wanted to wander inside.

He quickly dried his foot and wrapped it in a clean linen. Then he limped out into the narrow hall before treading downstairs.

A host of people, it seemed, had crowded themselves into the kitchen. Glykera stood near the counter as she poured hot water from the authepsa. Ianthe was beside her, holding a baby in her arms.

Was this one of her grandchildren?

His mother was sitting on a chair, but her head teetered as if she might tumble over. Instead of concern for the child, confusion filled her eyes.

Matthias waved his hand, taking charge like he was the captain of this ship. "Someone take that baby out of here."

Ianthe stepped toward the back door, but she didn't leave the kitchen.

Instead of echoing his command, Glykera opted to usurp the limits of his authority. "Help your mother," she said, steam billowing up from the cup in her hand.

Imma was listing like a ship that had run aground, the hull of her body about to sink onto the rush mat below. He knelt beside her and righted her with his shoulder.

She whispered something into his ear, words he couldn't understand.

He leaned closer. "What is it?"

"Matthias?" she asked, seemingly confused.

"Of course." Who else would it be?

"I'm not well."

"What happened?" he asked.

Instead of answering, she closed her eyes, leaning against him. He held her tight so she didn't slip off the chair.

Glykera spoke in lieu of his mother. "She walked up to the olive grove this morning. The sun, it seems, was too harsh."

But his mother had spent a lifetime in the Judean sun, walking along both the hills and shore. Something else was wrong. Glykera must know that she was ailing beyond the stroke of sun.

When the baby cried again, he knew he had to get Imma away from the noise of this child and the eyes of a crowd. Perhaps Niles could help him transport her upstairs so she could rest on her bed.

Korinna stepped into the kitchen, and when Ianthe saw the younger woman, she handed her the baby. For a moment, he forgot about his mother's affliction and focused on Korinna. Did she and Agathon already have a child? Perhaps that was why she refused to leave the man. She could have been hiding a baby from all of them.

But Korinna didn't welcome this baby to her chest. Instead she looked as surprised at the gift as Matthias had been when he stepped into the chaos of this room.

If it wasn't her child, who had brought this baby to them?

Korinna looked up at Matthias as if he might be able to help her understand what was happening, but he just shook his head. He would have to sort through the details later. Right now, he needed to focus on helping his mother heal.

Ianthe stepped up to him. "She needs to rest."

The woman was right, but this kitchen wasn't the place for her to sleep.

Ianthe placed her gnarled hand on his shoulder. "You've hurt yourself," she said softly, as if she knew not to alert the others.

He'd forgotten about his bandaged foot until it crept out from under the tunic.

"It's only a gash," he said, wanting to focus their attention back on helping Imma.

"Does it feel hot?" she asked.

"Only around the edges."

"I'll fetch some salt water to cleanse it," she said.

"After my mother is resting," he said. He didn't deserve her, or any, of their focus. "If we can't carry Imma upstairs, we need a mattress for her here."

His mother's head rested soundly against his shoulder. If he stepped away now, she'd topple over.

"I'll fetch the mattress," Niles said, taking a step toward the stairs.

"Thank you."

Glykera handed Matthias the cup of liquid, the steam cooled from the top now. "If you help her drink this, I'll carry the mattress with Niles."

Matthias lifted the ceramic to his mother's lips, and she took several sips. Imma had spent a lifetime caring for him, tending his wounds and brewing buckets of healing tea. It had never occurred to him that one day he might have to care for his mother.

Glykera had been right. He didn't know how to care for anyone but himself and he did that miserably. Perhaps it was time for him to learn how to care for both himself and those he loved.

The baby cried out again, a dismal sound that matched the limp state of her body. Is that what Matthias had looked like when Imma had found him?

His mother couldn't possibly care for anyone else. Not for a long time.

Ianthe turned away from him, focusing back on Korinna. "We need to find a wet nurse for that baby."

His mother muttered something, and Matthias moved closer to her ear. "What is it?"

"Diane," she whispered. The woman who had nursed him to health long ago.

Matthias dug two coins from his waist pouch, for Diane if she still fed children after these nineteen years.

He looked back at Korinna, who was cradling the baby close to her now. "Do you know of Diane?"

She shook her head.

Niles stepped into the room with the thin mattress, his wife close behind. "I will take you to her."

Ianthe nudged Korinna toward the door. "Please hurry."

Glykera laid the feather mattress to the side of the kitchen, and Matthias helped his mother rest on it. She stirred occasionally in the hour that passed, and when she opened her eyes, he gave her sips of Glykera's tea and rubbed the tincture from Ianthe into her temples.

As he waited beside his mother, Ianthe brought him a basin filled with warm water. Even though it stung, he settled his foot into it. Then she cleaned his wound and smeared clove oil on it before wrapping it again in a cloth.

He almost reached his hand out to pat her arm, thank her for her help, but he tucked it back under his sleeve lest she be as horrified by his defect as Korinna. He rarely used the hand, but whenever he was lax, most people backed away as if they feared he had leprosy.

He supposed he did have leprosy in a way, but not on his skin. The disease seemed to be somewhere deep inside him, eating away at any good.

The physician, Abel, interrupted them when he swept through the back door, dumping a pouchful of herbs onto the counter for Glykera to add to Imma's cinnamon tea. Then he examined her and concurred that she needed rest. No more buzzing around to prepare for the Rhapsodies or their community meetings. No more caring for anyone young or old until she was well herself.

Once her energy was restored, he thought the headaches would subside.

No one in this household, he said, was supposed to disturb Tabitha's rest. Especially a baby.

Korinna returned with the baby in time for Abel to pronounce it might yet live. When it started whimpering, Imma groaned in response, trying to inch up on the mattress.

Matthias insisted that she lie back down. He quickly saw Abel out and then turned to Korinna. "Did Diane feed her?"

"Yes."

"Then why is she still crying?"

"She's been through a lot. Look at her skin—"

Matthias didn't dare. "Can Diane keep her there?"

Korinna shook her head. "She's caring for two other children."

"She can stay here—" Imma started as she pushed herself up farther.

Matthias glanced up at Niles. "We have to get my mother upstairs."

The men helped Tabitha to her feet, and with Ianthe's clove oil to relieve some of his pain, Matthias was able to support her with both of his feet. With Imma's arms draped over their shoulders, they slowly crept up the stairs, the cries of the baby echoing behind them.

In his mother's chamber, Matthias helped her climb onto the mattress, filled with the softest wool. She settled into the pillows, closing her eyes. It was too hot to place a quilt over her now, but he would make sure that she was warm enough tonight.

She took his hand. "I'll be fine by evening."

"Abel said you're not allowed to get out of your bed until he gives his approval."

"I don't have time to stay in bed," she protested.

"But you must," he said. "We can't lose you, Imma. I can't lose you...."

"You won't lose me." She smiled at him. "We'll have an eternity together."

Terror struck his heart. Why was she speaking about the next life? These pains plaguing her, he feared, were more than the signs of exhaustion. Something else might be tormenting her head.

What if he, with all that he had done, was the reason her head wouldn't stop hurting?

He waited as she stirred on the pillows, trying to rest as the physician had ordered. After she slept, he kissed her forehead and moved back downstairs to decide what to do with this child. One thing was for certain, no matter what Imma said, the baby could not stay here. Not even when she was well again.

Korinna was waiting for him in the vestibule. She'd sunk to the floor, the baby resting now in her thin arms. When she looked up, Matthias slid down beside her like she'd done with him on the shore.

They were both adults in the eyes of their government, but this evening, it felt to him like they were two children trying to decide what to do with another child's life.

Korinna leaned back against the wall, gently bouncing the baby. "What are we going to do?"

"Perhaps Ianthe can care for her until we locate someone else to help."

She shook her head. "Ianthe can barely care for herself."

She was right, even if he didn't want to admit it. As much as he wanted to hand this child off to anyone who would take her, it couldn't be Ianthe.

"Where did my mother find her?" he asked.

"At the dump."

He took a deep breath, his mind adrift. How could he turn away a baby who had been abandoned like he had?

He dared to glance down into Korinna's arms, truly seeing this baby for the first time. He didn't know much about children, but it seemed that Korinna was right—her face was too red, skin parched from the sun. She had the black hair of a Hebrew girl, tiny curls that stuck to her forehead. Korinna had washed and salted her and swaddled her body in a white cloth.

"What shall we call her?" he asked.

Korinna smiled. "Hermione, I think."

*Daughter of the earth.* "It suits her," he said.

Korinna shifted the baby toward him. "Would you like to hold her?"

"No," he said, afraid to attach himself to this little one. "Would Diane care for her overnight if I paid extra?"

"She said she only feeds the babies."

Matthias pointed toward the ceiling. "Imma must sleep, and the baby will waken her."

"Perhaps Zoe or one of the other ladies from the community could help us."

The baby began to wiggle in spite of the rattling sound. Korinna placed her small finger into the baby's mouth so she could suck on it.

The woman before him, it seemed, knew exactly what to do with a child.

"You could take her home," he said.

Her green eyes widened. "Agathon will never let me keep a baby."

"Just for the night," he said. "I'll speak with Zoe in the morning, once Imma is well enough for me to leave."

She seemed to consider his words.

"I'll send money for the wet nurse and some extra for you."

She shook her head again. "I wouldn't do this for money."

He studied her. What kind of person didn't want money when it was offered? If anyone needed money, Korinna did.

"I want to find her a good home," she said. "And I want your mother to be well."

"Abel said the herbs and rest will cure the pain in her head." But perhaps not the pain in her heart when she found out what he did to Bethany.

Korinna gently removed her finger, cradling the baby in her arms. "I will pray for your mother."

"I don't believe in prayer."

"I suppose God can still answer, even if you don't believe."

He stood and reached down for her arm, helping her to stand. "Do you think God will relieve you from a marriage to Agathon?"

"Tabitha says that God might choose to work through the marriage instead."

He hoped, for Korinna's sake, that God—if He actually cared—would give her another option. And that God would choose to heal his mother so He could continue loving others through her life.

# CHAPTER EIGHTEEN

Mist settled over the city of Joppa that afternoon, blown in by the sea. Instead of returning home with Hermione, Korinna wandered the winding streets until it was time to visit the wet nurse again.

The baby ate ravenously from Diane's breast, as if she hadn't eaten four hours ago. Korinna waited on a stool and gazed out into the gray light of dusk, its brilliant colors erased in the haze. In her palm was a coin for Diane, and these stolen hours away from her prison, the power of this money to employ another, gave her a glimpse of what it might be like to be free.

"Bring her again at dawn," Diane instructed when Korinna left with the baby, and Korinna agreed. She would escort the baby one more time, then Matthias would have to hire another young woman to care for her.

But she would pretend, just for the night, that she had a baby. As long as Laurel would let the child stay in their house. If Laurel refused, she and Hermione would spend the night outside.

One day she would be faithful in caring for her own children. A cherished wife she'd never be, no matter how much she longed to be loved, but just perhaps, her children would love her as much as she loved them. As much as Matthias loved Tabitha.

Not that it mattered who cared for her on this earth. According to Tabitha, Korinna was loved by God, and His sacrifice had redeemed all that was wicked inside her. This God didn't want her to hate her master or envy others or worship the gods of Greece. This God—the Eternal One—wanted her to trust Him, to be His daughter.

A daughter.

The word washed over her like a rose-scented bath, cleansing her once again. Never in her life had she dreamed that she could become a daughter. At first Korinna hadn't believed God would care for a slave, but as the weeks passed, she saw the goodness of God and His love in the widows around her. They no longer had husbands—and some had no children—but they shone in the light of being a prized daughter of a king. He cared for them when society rejected them as worthless. Unclean.

"You are a daughter too," she whispered to the baby cuddled against her, content again from the milk. Hermione, she prayed, would know that she was a treasure, not a discarded piece of trash. While her parents might have abandoned her, her life was not an accident. Korinna prayed that God would bless her as a follower of His Way so she could be a blessing to others.

She began to climb the hill toward Agathon's house, passing by the villa of Simon the Tanner. The home of the woman whom Matthias adored. What a blessed woman Bethany was to be loved so deeply and not just by one man—by her father and husband and the man whose heart she had broken when she married Joshua.

A seed of jealousy floated through the foggy night, threatening to plant itself in the freshly turned soil of her heart. What would it be like to be loved by, to marry, a man who cared deeply like Matthias? Even more, what would it be like to be loved by a man who served God and cared for his wife?

She looked away from the clay walls of this villa, trying to pluck out the jealousy before it took root. If not, she knew well that bitterness could overwhelm her, and she wanted no bitterness now.

As she cradled Hermione, she prayed for Tabitha's and Bethany's healing. Then she petitioned God on behalf of Matthias, that he would experience the freedom that she and the disciples of the Way had found. That he would be content with who God made him, not in what he could conquer or obtain or who he could convince to love him back.

The lantern flames guided her in the darkness, and she slowed her steps, savoring these last moments outside with Hermione. Laurel might explode when she saw the baby, but she'd calm down when Korinna explained it was only for the night. She didn't have many chores for her while Agathon was gone anyway. The kitchen would be easy to sweep while Hermione rested on her mat.

When Agathon returned, they would all have plenty of work to occupy the house. Food was the one thing their master didn't bargain for—he wanted the best foods, prepared the way he liked to eat when visiting cities far from here. She'd be busy helping in the kitchen until their wedding.

Master. Husband.

Her position wouldn't change much, she suspected, when Agathon returned, except she'd be expected to give all of herself to him. Laurel said that Korinna would no longer have to assist in the kitchen or dispose of the chamber pots, although she'd continue doing those jobs quite willingly in lieu of becoming Agathon's wife. But she had no voice in this decision. Agathon owned her. He could do what he wanted.

She cringed at that thought, of what he might do in their marriage bed, but if she ran away, like Matthias suggested, Agathon would hunt her down. Her punishment would be severe.

When Selene was alive, Korinna hadn't feared him like other female slaves might fear their master. Selene had protected her youngest slave with her life and made Agathon promise to keep her chaste until Korinna married. Selene also asked Agathon to find a husband for Korinna and set her free.

Agathon had found her a husband in himself and kept his promise to keep her chaste, but he'd never intended to set her free. A free woman, she suspected, wouldn't agree to marry him. Not willingly. She was his only hope of birthing an heir.

A thought began growing in her mind, the hope of freedom in the midst of this arranged marriage. Agathon might own her body, but God was now the gatekeeper of her soul. She could worship Him at home, sing the psalms in her heart if not with her voice. Or she could sing like Bethany when Agathon was out at sea, the melody and words sustaining her.

How she hoped her husband would allow her to continue attending the gatherings. Perhaps she could keep sewing with Tabitha, bringing any children that she would birth to play among the flowers and birds in the peace of her courtyard. And she would do her best, with God's help, to respect a man who seemed impossible to love.

When she stepped through the back door, into the kitchen, Laurel's eyes fell to the baby.

"Where did you get that?" the older woman barked, pointing at her arms as if Korinna had stolen a piece of old leather from Simon's stall.

She edged back the swaddling cloth so Laurel could see Hermione's face. "She was abandoned in the dump. Matthias asked me to—"

Before she finished speaking, Laurel grabbed Hermione and dropped the baby into a basket of linens, covering it quickly with a woven lid. Startled, Korinna lunged for the basket. While she'd known the staff might not be pleased with hosting a baby for the night, she'd hoped Laurel would respect her choice as Agathon's betrothed.

"What are you—" Korinna didn't finish. The slap of sandals in the passage, the sound of stomping feet, silenced her.

Agathon had returned from his voyage.

The man's eyes were wild when he scanned the kitchen, his normally kempt hair in disarray. He was never in a good mood when he returned from a trip, but this was different. A fury inside him had resurfaced. In the past, only Selene could calm this rage.

After a voyage, Selene would plan a grand feast with all his favorite foods, and sometimes they even hosted guests to welcome him back. But no one was celebrating now, especially not her. None of the staff knew what was to come next except that they'd all be tethered in the chaos that Agathon brought home with him.

Ignoring Laurel, he stepped toward Korinna. "Where have you been?"

"With Tabitha…"

"Glykera told me you left hours ago."

She glanced at the basket below his waist, knowing that she couldn't possibly say anything about Hermione. He'd insist that she return this baby to the dump, and she could never do that.

"Did you go someplace with Matthias—"

"Of course not." She'd been faithful to Agathon this past month, in her body if not in her heart.

He towered over her, his fists clenched, and she feared what he might do in his anger.

"I—" Her gaze fell to the ground, to the woven threads of the basket as she struggled to find her voice. "Tabitha needed me for an errand."

He pounded the wall. "I never should have let you sew with her."

She felt the walls of the small corner she'd created inside herself start to crumble, filling up all the spaces where she'd had room to breathe.

"My wedding garment," she said, trying to deter him. "It's almost finished."

"I don't care about a tunic—"

"I've learned so much from her about sewing and managing a household and freedom...."

The moment she said the last word, she knew it was a mistake. A rush of flames blazed across his ruddy cheeks. "Freedom?"

"Through the Messiah." She rubbed her bare arms even though the kitchen air was warm. "Not from your service."

"You are never to visit Dorcas's home again!"

Every remnant of wall that she'd built seemed to crash down. "But—"

A cry rose between them, and she stared down at the basket in horror. If only she could lift it and run, like Matthias, to an island far from here. Surely she and Hermione could find a place to hide.

"I will help Laurel prepare a meal," she blurted, grasping for a way to convince him to leave this room. But Laurel seemed to have disappeared from the kitchen, leaving Korinna and Hermione to face his wrath alone.

"What is that sound?" he demanded.

Words began cascading from her mouth, explaining what they could make him for his supper, praying she could distract him with the temptation of food. Pear compote boiled in wine and honey. Smoked lamb. His favorite salad made of coriander and mint and pine sauce.

"Quiet, Korinna."

"But—"

He silenced her again, tilting his head to listen until his gaze latched onto the basket. "It sounds like a baby crying."

It was unbearable, the thought of exposing this infant to his anger, but Hermione revealed herself with another cry.

Agathon shoved Korinna aside and lifted the lid. He turned back to her, the rage in his eyes lapsed into curiosity. Interest, even.

"Is it a boy?" he asked, a bit of wonder overpowering the disdain.

Her voice was quiet when she spoke again. She feared what he would do with the truth. "A girl."

He dropped the lid, the hardness crusting his face again. "Is it yours?"

"Of course not."

He took another step closer to her, the cries growing louder. "Whose baby is it?"

"I don't know."

Agathon lifted his arm, and she braced herself. The back of his hand, the weight of his rings, whipped across her face, and she cried out like the baby as pain shot through her head. She backed away, her arms a shield, humiliated at the assault of a man who was supposed to protect her as a wife.

He raised his hand again. "Where did you get this child?"

"Tabitha found her in the dump."

He lifted the basket lid a second time and threw it across the room. Then he plucked Hermione out of the safety of those cloths and held her out as if she were a bedpan in need of dumping.

Korinna reached out her arms. "I'll take her back."

"I'll return her to Dorcas myself." Hermione in his hands, he stomped out the back door and vanished into the fog.

She fell to her knees and prayed to the one God whom she'd chosen just yesterday to serve. Prayed for mercy on the life of this baby girl.

If Agathon would truly take her back to Tabitha, someone—Matthias or Glykera—would surely find a place for her to thrive.

# CHAPTER NINETEEN

The coolness slipping through Tabitha's window was a blessed relief for her head, along with the many remedies that God had provided through those who cared for her. Abel told her to rest, but sleep had retreated for the night along with the sun. Now the evening air beckoned her outside.

Even with her energy drained, Tabitha was grateful beyond words that she had climbed the hill above Joppa. God had known that someone was going to leave that baby girl, and she was glad, humbled, that He had called her to a place she never would have gone in the shape she'd been in. Glad that He'd been able to use her life in the midst of it.

She pushed back the quilt someone had placed over her, wishing she could see the stars. Reaching for a cup on the bedside pedestal, she then guzzled the remaining tea, mixed with a potent mixture of herbs. Her thirst for water and air alike drove her to step onto the floor and tiptoe across the stones so she didn't awaken Glykera, who slept on a mat nearby to assist her.

In the kitchen below, she retrieved spring water from a bucket and drank the entire cup before moving slowly to the courtyard, her hand on the side of the wall to balance in the dark.

Instead of a display of stars as she'd hoped, most of the stars were hidden behind a covering of clouds. Disappointed, she eased down on the divan nearest the birdbath, longing for a glimpse of God and His handiwork. Even though she couldn't see beyond the clouds, He was here. Still she wanted so badly to see His beauty in the midst of suffering, the silver threads that stitched all that He was doing together for good.

Instead everything in her mind seemed as cloudy as the sky.

But she would trust in His goodness, His faithfulness, in spite of all that pressed up against her. He was here even when she couldn't see Him, directing like He had when He called her up the hill.

The front door to the house opened, the door banging against the vestibule wall, and her heart stilled. In all the confusion tonight, someone must have forgotten to latch it. Did one of her ladies need help? They had few intruders in their neighborhood, but it wasn't beyond possibility. She didn't have the strength to shout if a thief came into the courtyard, but an intruder wouldn't find much of worth here to steal beyond fabric and thread.

A shadow moved across the entrance, and Tabitha held her breath until she heard the cry of a baby.

"Korinna?" she called out, her voice so weak that it barely carried beyond the trickle of the birdbath.

"It's not Korinna."

She cringed at the voice of the man she knew well. Why was Agathon here?

He stepped into the courtyard, and while she couldn't see the baby girl, she assumed that he carried her.

"You've returned," she said simply, pressing herself up to her feet. It wouldn't do for Agathon to see her in a sickly state. Instead of compassion, he would lord this illness over her.

With God's help, she would show him the strength that she held only in the Messiah.

A small, tentative step ahead and then she forced a second and third one until she reached the birdbath. Leaning against the basin, she propped herself up against the stone so he wouldn't see her weakness.

"I came home to find a baby in my house," he said, his tone like frost.

Tabitha wished that she could reach out and comfort the crying baby, but she could barely support herself.

"Then my slave claims to have found freedom in your Messiah."

The details of this past week remained fuzzy in her mind, but she remembered the joy of praying with Korinna, this answer to her own prayer when Korinna had decided to follow Christ.

"She is not free from you, Agathon. It is a freedom of her heart."

"She will never be free!" he shouted.

With this noise, spit spewed into her face, and another wave of pain blasted through her head. "You can be free as well—"

"I am free."

"Sell Korinna to me," she said, desperation rising inside her. "Then you won't have to marry—"

"I will marry whom I please," he said. "And soon I will have a son."

He shoved the crying baby toward her, dropping the girl into her arms.

The press of this child, the weakness in her ankles, it was too much to withstand. Her unsteady legs gave way to the weight; legs that had been faithful for forty-three years would hold her no longer.

Darkness pulled her downward, but she couldn't take this infant with her. Her back arched forward and her body clammed over itself like a shell, the cast of anchors pulling her into the depths. She prayed in those seconds as she fell for mercy on this child. For mercy on all those she loved.

Another pain jabbed her head, pounding against her skull. As her body curled on the bed of lavender and hyacinths, she heard the muffled cry of the baby.

Thank God—He had saved the girl.

Someone took the child from her arms, and she opened her eyes again, her vision blurry.

A curse and then Agathon knelt on the ground beside her. "Dorcas?" he urged. "Tabitha…"

She wanted to answer, to tell him that she no longer despised him for all he'd done, that the Messiah could redeem his story as well. But her mouth didn't seem to work.

Agathon shouted for help, but no one in this household, as much as they loved her, could rescue her with their onions or ointment or herbs. When God called His children home, they didn't dare refuse.

"God loves you, Agathon. No matter what." As her eyes closed again, she reached out, taking a hand. Agathon's, she hoped.

"Tabitha—"

"I forgive you," she managed to whisper. "For everything."

Another curse escaped his lips, but this word quickly faded into the strain of music. The loveliest song she'd ever heard. A lyre, perhaps, though she'd never heard such a beautiful melody on its strings.

Then a flicker of light—she saw it ahead in the darkness. Only a glimmer, but it was a flame of hope. The end of her journey.

Someone took her hand, and she knew, more assured than she'd ever been, that God did indeed love her. Only a loving Father would await His daughter on the other side of the darkness, welcoming her to the place beyond.

A place she knew in her heart was home.

# CHAPTER TWENTY

Matthias shot like an arrow into the courtyard. He'd heard Imma's cry, and in the dim light he could see her lying on the ground, Agathon at her side.

Why was his ailing mother in the courtyard with this vile man?

Matthias grabbed Agathon's shoulder, yanking him back. "What have you done?"

The merchant shook his head, his voice broken. "She hit her head on the side of the bath."

Matthias folded onto the ground, cradling his mother. He couldn't see any blood in the darkness, but he felt the stickiness on his hands, the glue matted to her hair.

A thousand questions collided in his mind. Why was his mother down in the courtyard instead of safe in her bed? How did she fall? And why was Agathon calling in the night?

"Imma." He spoke quietly at first and then Matthias said her name louder as if he might waken her. He didn't want to hurt her, but still he shook, yearning for her to respond.

When she didn't stir, he wanted to punch something. Someone.

And then run away on the next ship out of Joppa.

But he couldn't leave now. He had to take care of his mother.

He glanced over at Agathon. "Did you push her?"

"No, I—" He stopped. "Korinna brought home a baby. I was returning it."

The child rested in Agathon's arms, her voice as still now as Imma's. Matthias could only imagine what the man might have done in his fury. Agathon didn't like his mother caring for women like Korinna or taking a portion of his profit whenever he returned to Joppa, but would he try to kill her?

The merchant had insisted Isaac go out into a storm long ago to fix his ship. Now he'd brought a storm right into Isaac's home.

A lantern flared to his right as Niles circled the courtyard with a torch to set the other lanterns ablaze. The light they needed to care for Imma.

"It was an accident," Agathon said. "I never meant—"

"Go find Abel!" Matthias commanded.

He held up the bundle. "But this baby—"

"I'll take her," Glykera said, her arms outstretched.

Moments after handing over the child, Agathon was gone.

"Does my mother know?" he asked Glykera.

The woman glanced up from the baby. "Know what?"

"About what I did to Bethany in the market—"

"Everyone knows what happened, Matthias."

"And it broke her...."

"Her head has been hurting for a long time," Glykera said before turning away.

But the pain, he was certain, had increased since he'd returned. She had said that she wanted him here, but what pain he'd caused. A mortal wound, he feared, this time.

As he waited, his mother's head resting in his lap, Matthias prayed to Imma's God. If He was real, if He was good, Matthias begged Him to save his mother's life. She was needed here in Joppa, for decades ahead of them. To help this baby and the ladies she loved. To help so many…

When Abel and Agathon returned, they found Matthias still bent over his mother, still praying even though he felt no breath in her. He couldn't bear to examine the wound himself. Even Glykera, who'd been so determined to treat Imma with her onion packs and tea, didn't offer a remedy. She'd given up, Matthias feared. But none of them could give up now. They had to fight for Imma's life.

Abel examined her in the lantern light, and when he rose from the ground, Matthias could see the deep sadness in his gaze, the hope vanquished.

Matthias tried to cling to the hope that remained in him. "She will recover?"

"I'm sorry, son."

An apology was not acceptable. He wanted assurance, the promise of life.

"Ianthe has a tincture—" he started.

"No tincture will bring her back to us."

The fog in his mind obscured the man's words.

"Then pray," Matthias said. "For God to heal her."

When Abel shook his head, Matthias fingered the hem of his garment. "I can't lose my mother."

The physician lifted his pouch off the ground. "I'm afraid it's too late to get what you want, Matthias."

Grief paralyzed him, his limbs and tongue. It couldn't be too late.

"You'll have to bury her today," Abel said.

"It's not too late!"

"Matthias—"

He stood and backed away from Abel's outstretched hand. This man was wrong. They were all wrong.

"I'll pay for everything," Agathon said as Matthias stepped back, the courtyard spinning around him. He had to get outside these walls, far away from here.

He limped out of the courtyard, into the fog. Waves crashed into the rocks by the harbor, shooting up water. He lifted a stone from the beach and hurled it into the air. He couldn't hear the stone drop, couldn't see it land, but he knew it had sunk to the sea floor.

He heaved another stone into the sea and then another, wishing the grief inside him would sweep away in the waves. His mother couldn't be gone. God—the God of resurrection, who'd raised His own Son from the grave, could surely have healed her.

Why hadn't He saved Imma from death?

He threw one more stone and then sank onto the ground.

One wave could wash over him in a moment, swallowing the pain inside him. Taking him away before he hurt someone else.

He'd tried to take Bethany from Joshua because he thought he still loved her, but he had done it because he was selfish. Afraid, even, of those he had loved no longer loving him. Now when they buried Imma today, his stupidity and insolence would put his own mother in the grave.

God help him, he'd wronged those he loved in a quest to overcome his fear.

He was sorry, sorry to his core, but it was too late to tell his mother now. Forgiveness was extended to the living, not the dead. The God of resurrection could have…

*The God of resurrection.*

The words washed through his mind like the waves over his feet.

His whole life he'd heard how God could raise people like Lazarus from the dead. How He'd ultimately conquered death by bringing His Son back from the grave. If only this God that Imma loved would bring her back into this world for a season. If only He'd show that He was more powerful than the gods in Greece or beyond. That He was really the God of the living as well as the dead.

The waves splashing over him, Matthias prayed that God was indeed real and that He would demonstrate His power in their lives.

That His needle would stitch back together the wounds that Matthias had caused.

Resurrect them all.

Agathon cursed an entire host of Greek gods in his chamber, the profanity bleeding out the open windows. Korinna had heard profanity from her master's mouth plenty of times, but not like this. His anger shook the plaster walls, sending tremors down her chest.

What had he done with Hermione?

Pacing across her small room, she listened for the cry of a baby but none came, so she sank to her knees on the cold stone, begging God to keep this child safe. Then she asked God to redeem whatever had happened during the night, just as He had redeemed her life. According to Tabitha, the Messiah had loved even His enemies. She'd said the God of miracles, the impossible, could redeem anyone.

Her knees pressed into the stone, she continued to pray, but Agathon's anger only seemed to escalate with her prayers. Perhaps God needed to break him in order to build him back up again.

Agathon must choose his own course, but Hermione still needed someone to help her.

Come morning, Korinna wouldn't be able to leave the house, but she could leave now, if only for an hour, to make sure that the baby was in a safe place. After his voyage, Agathon would surely sleep late. Only Laurel would know she was gone.

Lifting herself from her knees, she prayed again that God would redeem whatever had happened overnight. And she prayed that she would be able to find Hermione before dawn.

# CHAPTER TWENTY-ONE

Matthias would never be welcome back inside Simon's house, but still he pounded on the front door. He needed to speak with this man before they took Imma's body up to the grave.

"Simon!" he shouted to the windows, blood spiraling through his veins. Even if he didn't want anything to do with Matthias, he would want to help the woman who had been the backbone of their community.

The man finally leaned out of an upper window, a lamp in his hand. "I told you to leave Bethany alone."

"I need to speak with you," Matthias called. "It's urgent—"

"Go home, Matthias," he said, the light disappearing back into the shadows.

"Please, Simon…"

Moments later the man opened the door, dawn trickling into the entryway. "What's wrong?"

"My mother—" he started but choked on the words. Somehow speaking the truth felt like wrapping the first length of burial cloth around her broken body, something he could never unwrap. Still the man before him needed to know in order to pray for a miracle. "She's dead, Simon. She was unwell, and then during the night, she fell and hit her head."

Simon collapsed back against the doorpost, the fight draining out of him. "I'm sorry."

Sorrow rushed out of Matthias in his tears, the acknowledgment of all that had gone wrong.

"We must gather the community to bury her," Simon said.

A fresh courage rose up in Matthias as he shook his head. "You must pray that your God brings her back to life."

Simon shook his head. "I'm not a healer, Matthias."

"But your God—"

"This death is only a passing for your mother. She is with Elohim now. Healed in the next life."

"She is still needed here. No one helps the women in Joppa like she does."

"Someone will take her place."

He shook his head. "Who?"

Simon had no answer because he knew, as Matthias did, that their community needed this woman of faith.

"Someone in Joppa must be willing to pray for a resurrection," he said.

"Matthias—"

He shook his head. "Your God is supposed to be more powerful than a pantheon of gods, but you won't even ask Him for a miracle."

The Rhapsodies had already gathered before Matthias arrived home, their cries streaming out into the street like the priests who lamented in Jerusalem's temple. The women had helped Niles relocate Tabitha to the upper room so they could wash her skin and then prepare the body for burial with the oils of lavender and myrrh.

He couldn't bear to join them, couldn't bear to see the wound that had bled out in his hands. Nor could he see the body of this woman who'd loved him dearly without life in her lungs or a smile on her lips to welcome him home.

*I cried by reason of mine affliction unto the Lord, and he heard me; out of the belly of hell cried I, and thou heardest my voice.*

The words he'd learned long ago from Jonah, when the prophet was a fugitive caught in the body of a great fish. When everyone else thought he was dead. Like Jonah, Matthias felt as if he was trapped in the shackles of hell. He wished there truly was a God powerful enough to deliver him.

Tears clouding his vision, Matthias changed into his sleeveless traveling cloak with a hood to protect his head from the sun. Then he rubbed Ianthe's clove oil on his wounded foot and wrapped it once again before he tied the straps on his sandals. Inside his pouch was the handful of coins needed to drown his grief. His destination was irrelevant. Any place was better than here, watching the elders transport his mother up to a cave.

Never again would Imma wait for him by the quay. Hold out her arms to welcome him home. Never again would she sew him another tunic as her offering of love.

He limped toward the kitchen to pack some provisions for his journey. As he entered the room, he saw Korinna on a chair, the baby asleep in her arms. When she saw his face, she placed Hermione on a bed of linens and opened her arms.

He sank into her, his sorrow pouring out on the stone floor. Then he backed away, horrified at himself for seeking comfort in her arms. Korinna was betrothed to another man, like Bethany had been. For him to bare himself to another woman, on the very day his mother was being laid out for burial... He would bring dishonor to his family one more time.

"I'm sorry." He wiped his tears on his cloak. "I didn't mean to—"

"You've done nothing wrong, Matthias," she said. "I am your friend."

He began stuffing dried fruit and cheese into his pouch, and Korinna's eyes widened with concern. "Where are you going?"

"As far away as possible."

"You can't run, Matthias."

"I have to…"

"You can run," a man said behind him, "as long as you run to Lydda first."

Matthias swiveled on his bad foot, the pain burning up his leg.

Simon was under the archway dressed in a camel's hair cloak, a purse hanging from his sash. He held up a wooden crutch in his hand. "I thought you might need this."

Matthias didn't take it. "For what?"

"Peter the Apostle is still in Lydda. The elders have asked us to find him."

The pestle in his mind slowly crushed the words. Lydda was a full day's walk. Did the elders think Peter might pray for a miracle?

"But you don't believe—" Matthias stopped, eyeing Korinna. He couldn't say the words about God raising his mother. It would sound ludicrous to her ears.

"I didn't say that, Matthias. We can always ask, but I don't believe He responds to our demands."

He considered the words. The winds of the sea blew where they would, but he'd spent much of his past year trying to ride them, not knowing exactly where he'd land. If he was going to run somewhere, he might as well go to Lydda. Perhaps this Peter could pray.

He turned back to Korinna. To allow a body to sit for more than a day was disrespectful for both the deceased and their family, but he needed her to understand. "Please don't let them bury my mother while we're gone. We'll only be two days—three at the most."

"And you will return?" she asked.

He nodded solemnly.

"Then I'll ask them not to bury her until you're home."

Simon waved him toward the door. "We better start walking so we have enough light."

Matthias took the crutch, then glanced at Korinna one last time. She gifted him with the strength of her smile. Wings he needed to fly swiftly to Lydda and back again.

He and Simon would find this apostle and bring him to Joppa.

# CHAPTER TWENTY-TWO

A dreary sadness had banked itself over Tabitha's house as the Rhapsodies mourned their loss. While the women sang through the Psalms, Korinna helped Ianthe and the others prepare the body with oils and perfumes. Then she placed a wreath of flowers on Tabitha's head.

Zoe shrouded the body with purple linen from Galilee, the finest material she owned, and the women took turns watching over their dear sister in the upper room, the villa's lime-coated roof damp from their tears. It seemed as if the entire city showed up to mourn their loss, bringing mounds of fruit as gifts to fill up Glykera's kitchen.

When Abel suggested they carry Tabitha's body up to the grave this morning, before someone else grew ill from whatever had plagued her, Korinna reminded him that both Simon the Tanner and Tabitha's son left strict instructions that the body remain here until they returned for the funeral.

Korinna didn't know why the men needed Peter to pray now that Tabitha was gone, but her friend would have been pleased to know that Matthias was willing to pray. Now Korinna prayed that Matthias would keep his word and return home, that what happened to his mother wouldn't send him away forever.

Abel and the Hebrew leaders in Joppa gave Simon and Matthias until the end of the Sabbath to return. At first light on Sunday, whether or not the men were home, Tabitha's body would be carried up to the cave where her husband had been laid to rest.

Korinna kept watch beside Tabitha's bed with Hermione asleep in her arms, the aromas of myrrh, cinnamon, and aloe spice covering the stench. Agathon wouldn't let her keep the baby, but Laurel had sent her over yesterday to help Glykera with whatever she needed. Most of all, Glykera needed help caring for Hermione, and Korinna was more than happy to comply. She'd even spent the night at Tabitha's home so she could carry Hermione to the wet nurse in the early morning hours.

The blisters on Hermione's face and arms had started to heal with the oils that Ianthe gave her. What would happen to her now that Tabitha was gone? The Rhapsodies planned to continue selling their wares at the stall for as long as possible, but none of them had the means to care for a baby.

While she didn't have the ability to care for a baby either, Korinna would protect her for as long as she was able. Once Matthias returned, after they buried his mother, they would discuss what to do with Hermione.

The shock of losing Tabitha sank deep inside her. Was her friend being punished for inviting a pagan like she was to enter into the kingdom of God? Tabitha said everyone was welcome, but perhaps God didn't want a slave. She longed for His truth, the beauty and kindness that she'd seen in Tabitha's life, but maybe she still wasn't good enough for Him.

Hermione began to stir, and Korinna shifted the girl in her arms. From below, the worship of the community began to rise up to the room, a sorrowful sound as they riffled their way through another psalm without Bethany's lyre. Nothing, it seemed, would lift the spirits that had sunk this church like a vessel crashed into the shore.

Zoe stepped into the room and placed her hand on Korinna's shoulders. "I will take over the watch."

"I can wait here," Korinna said even though she longed to be among the living below, to hear why God might have taken this servant from them.

Zoe pulled a second wooden chair beside her. "We all need to rest and worship in the midst of our sadness."

Korinna stood slowly, Hermione in her arms.

"Would you like me to hold her?" Zoe asked.

Korinna shook her head. For now, for this day and perhaps another if Agathon allowed it, she would care for this child as if she were her own. Like Tabitha, in their hours together, had cared for her.

She and Hermione sat on a divan around the perimeter of the courtyard as the dwindling community, only a dozen or so now, worshipped together.

Then Joshua began to speak. "The Messiah went before Tabitha to prepare a place for her and all of us. While we're sad, we need not mourn. God has prepared a home for her, and we will continue here in Joppa, following in His Way and His will."

Joshua didn't mention Matthias, but she prayed for the lost man who intrigued and worried her alike. And she prayed that this Peter would come to encourage them all.

After Joshua finished speaking, the group slipped out of the courtyard silently, reverently, until only she and Ianthe remained. The older woman stepped slowly up to Korinna and looked down at the baby lingering between them.

"Matthias said that you carried her down the hill," Korinna said.

The woman's eyes grew damp, tears pooling in them.

Korinna kissed her cheek. "You saved her life."

"God's mercy to me."

Korinna eyed her curiously. "What do you mean?"

"A long time ago, I lost someone very precious."

Korinna held up the baby. "Would you like to hold her?"

Ianthe nodded slowly before sitting beside Korinna on the divan. She slowly lifted her arms, curling them into a cradle, and Korinna set the baby girl inside.

Ianthe gazed down as if she'd found a diamond buried in the rubbish pile. "She's beautiful, isn't she?"

"Very," Korinna said, the sadness lingering. Not only did this baby's parents abandon her, but Tabitha wouldn't be here to watch her grow. "Who did you lose, Ianthe?"

The woman paused before speaking again. "My son."

Korinna sighed with her older friend, the desire to know her own mother tugging on her heart. "No mother should ever lose her child."

"I didn't lose him exactly." When the older woman looked back at her, tears were trapped between the lines on her face. "I left him."

Left, not lost. Korinna shuddered at the words.

"I birthed him later in my life. I didn't have a husband anymore, you see. One of the Roman soldiers…" She shook her head as if it would clear her mind.

"That is a terrible fate…."

"I'd spent much of my life as a healer, helping others, but after that…I couldn't care for my own son. I was starving and so was he. I had no milk left within me and no money to pay for a nurse."

Korinna's voice trembled when she asked the next question. "Where did you leave him?"

"In the dump above Joppa."

"And so you returned—"

"I know he's gone, but his spirit lingers in my heart. When I'm there, I almost feel as if he is close." Her arms shook as she began to cry, Hermione whimpering with her. "God forgive me."

Korinna took the baby from her. "I believe He already has."

"I could think of no other way."

She began pacing the floor to comfort Hermione. "Tabitha said you have a sister near here."

Ianthe nodded. "She and her husband have little use for me and I can't fault them for it, but they let me sleep at their home, as long as I am gone for the daytime hours. It is a gift for me to have a place to rest. So many others don't have even that."

Korinna wouldn't have a place to sleep if it weren't for Agathon. Even if she was a slave, at least she had a place to live. Her heart longed for more, but perhaps she, like Ianthe, should be thankful for what she had.

Closing her eyes, she wondered what Tabitha would say in response, but instead of Tabitha's voice, she seemed to hear another. A voice someplace deep within her that spoke truth into her heart. A voice that said she belonged.

"I wish none of us," she finally said, "had to suffer through the loss of those we love.

"Instead of just mourning what we've lost, we must remember all the good left in this world. All the good that God has done through the hands of our sister."

She prayed that Matthias and Simon would return by tomorrow, so they could remember with their community the good that Tabitha had embraced in her life. The redemption of making new all that was broken in their world.

If not, others from their church would carry her body up the hill on a pallet, the morning after the Sabbath, to the olive grove above Joppa.

The place where God spoke to Tabitha through the trees.

# CHAPTER TWENTY-THREE

Word about Peter and his miracles had spread through the bustling town of Lydda, but Simon and Matthias couldn't seem to find the apostle.

They searched for hours among the many shops of craftsmen in this fertile valley—masters of cloth and leather and metal who created all manner of supplies for travelers and those who bought goods to deliver by caravan across Israel. Because it was a town that most people passed quickly through, on their journey to someplace like Jerusalem they deemed more important, those whom Matthias spoke with thought Peter must have moved on as well.

But neither Matthias nor Simon would stop looking. If Peter had continued to another town, someone from the church here would surely know where he'd traveled.

The clove oil that Ianthe had rubbed into Matthias's foot had worn off yesterday. With the heat on his skin, the redness that seemed to brighten by the hour, he couldn't search much longer. A colonnade offered a bit of respite from the midday sun, and as travelers with their carts and donkeys passed by, the dust stirring in clouds around him, Matthias leaned against a column and reflected back on their journey.

Neither he nor Simon spoke as they traversed the rocky hills into this valley—Plain of Sharon—that bloomed crimson in the summer. While each step hurt, he never complained. Simon knew more than anyone that Matthias deserved this pain. He never should have approached Bethany in the market, but more than that, he never should have assumed in his pride that Bethany would want to leave her husband to be with him.

What a wretched man he was to think that he could have this woman who wasn't his.

He deserved this pain in his foot, in his heart, but his mother hadn't done anything wrong. God had released His anger—His vengeance—on the wrong person.

All along their journey through the hills, the foolishness of this quest, the desperate desire to breathe life back into his mother's lips, plagued him. What if no one, not even Elohim—this God above other gods—could overcome death?

The stories he'd heard as a boy about resurrection seemed contrived by people who needed to believe in *something*. Who, like him, couldn't bear to be wrong. The disciples had worshipped a man-god who'd died, and they refused to let go of this fallacy lest their own existence, what they had devoted their lives to, proved false.

He'd chosen not to worship a specific god, but he'd devoted his life to Bethany. She'd become like one of the idols on the acropolis inside him, and then this idol had crumbled into rubble, his heart along with it.

Even if Elohim couldn't overcome death in this world, could He bring any good out of the rubble?

Simon moved ahead without Matthias, stopping under an archway of another shop to inquire about Peter.

"You've wounded yourself," someone said.

A man moved into the shade beside Matthias, his full beard and dusty tunic the wardrobe of one on a journey. A traveler, Matthias assumed, passing through to a seaport or the city of Jerusalem. Or, perhaps, a thief in search of a victim.

Matthias checked for his purse, buried in the folds of his garment. Then he tucked his bandaged foot back under the hem of his robe. "It's healing...."

"I'm not talking about the cut on your foot." The older man smiled at him in kindness. "I'm speaking about the wounds in your heart."

Matthias's eyes grew wide. "You're Peter—the one we're looking for!"

"No one should search for me," the man said. "They should search for the God I serve."

"The God who raised His Son from the grave?"

The man's laughter faded as he studied Matthias. "Why have you come looking for me?"

"My mother has died—" The words drained the little strength he had left. "My mother believed your God could raise people from the dead, and I've come with an elder from our church to ask that He raise her from her grave, like He did with Lazarus."

Matthias braced himself for the man's scorn, but Peter didn't laugh again. Instead he directed him into a shop where two men were smithing iron over a fire.

"What do you believe?" Peter asked.

Smoke settled over them like the haze in his mind. "I don't know—"

"I was there the day Jesus called Lazarus out of the grave," Peter said. "He did it to reveal the greatness and glory of His Father and to build the faith of His Church."

Matthias had never met someone who had seen this Jesus perform a miracle, and the reality made his heart race. Perhaps the stories he'd heard were true. "My mother wanted nothing more than to build up His Church."

"Who is your mother?" Peter asked.

"Tabitha," he replied. "And she loved Elohim and His Son more than anything. The people of Joppa need her."

Peter eyed him for a moment. "Do the people need her, or do you?"

"I—" And the tears that Matthias had been fighting, tears that no respectable man would ever show a stranger, flowed down his cheeks, no breakwater to stop them. "We all need her."

"Only Jesus can mend the broken pieces inside you." Peter glanced over at the metalsmith. "Sometimes He even uses fire to do the shaping and mending. The fire that burns can also heal."

That's what Imma and the others had been telling him for years, but in order for him to trust, he had to step into an unknown place that was much more terrifying than traveling across a sea filled with fierce monsters. More terrifying than facing off a storm on the Mediterranean. It meant giving up control—of his life, his desires, the sin that plagued him.

"I was once much like you," Peter said. "A stone tossed by the sea until Jesus plucked me out of the water and set me high on a cliff. The waves still batter me, but I've burrowed myself into the Rock so they won't sweep me away again."

Matthias wanted to have that kind of faith, the strength of a cliff under his feet instead of the rocking back and forth.

"You have to decide," Peter said. "Will you believe in God's goodness, in His eternal love for you and your mother, even if He doesn't raise her from the grave?"

The flames warmed Matthias's back as the infection burned in his foot. Could he believe in Elohim—the one true God—even if he had to bury Imma? Could he trust what he couldn't see?

Through the open window, he saw a woman holding a child as Korinna had been holding the baby rescued from the dump, as Imma had once held him. She had shown him every day the goodness and the love of God even when he'd fought it. Even when he didn't think anyone except Bethany could love him.

Or perhaps he had to prove that someone like Bethany could love him—could heal his brokenness—when really he craved something much deeper. A love that could bring his heart back to life. A love that meant he didn't have to control the circumstances on his own. A love that didn't care if he was Hebrew or Greek.

His fortress crumbled in that moment. In the shadow of the apostle, in the flame that seemed to burn through him, Matthias knew this God of Peter's, the God of Simon and Imma, had the power to heal broken hearts and burn away the ashes to reveal the strength of bronze or iron inside. And He had the power to revive those who'd slipped into eternity.

"I want to believe," Matthias said. "No matter what happens to my mother, I want to believe in the goodness of your God."

"Not my God," Peter said gently. "The God we both now serve."

Simon entered the metalsmith's shop, his gaze wary as he studied Matthias talking to this stranger.

"It's Peter," Matthias said, stepping forward. Then he looked back up at the apostle in shock.

Lifting the hem of his garment, Matthias stared down at his foot. The redness had vanished, the gash stitched back together without ointment or the needle of a physician. The pain completely gone.

"God gives good gifts to His children," Peter told him before turning to Simon. "I've heard that Greek and Hebrew alike are worshipping together in the Joppa community."

"It's a small group," Simon said, "but we welcome anyone who wants to learn about our Savior."

Peter studied him for a moment before responding. "I will go with you to Joppa. To encourage your church."

"And my mother?" Matthias asked.

"I will pray as God leads," he said. "Her life and her death are in His hands."

And Matthias would pray as well, that God would lead his mother back into this life.

# CHAPTER TWENTY-FOUR

Korinna wrapped her arms around her legs, rocking herself in the shadows of her small chamber. Glykera had insisted on caring for Hermione tonight so Korinna could rest, but worry had stolen her sleep.

In these lonely hours, she prayed that Hermione would find a loving home and be raised by a family. And she prayed for Matthias, that the loss of his mother wouldn't force him deeper into his shell. He might want to be independent, but he needed others. And so did she, no matter how hard she fought it. She needed community outside this house void of any love.

Agathon's curses had silenced, but she hadn't seen him since Tabitha died. Instead of demanding extravagant meals, he'd secluded himself in his chamber. As far as she knew, the cargo that he'd brought from Greece was still on his ship, waiting to be transported into Jerusalem.

Tomorrow was Sunday. At dawn, the church would gather to say goodbye to the woman they loved, and nothing that Korinna could say would stop them from proceeding. They'd mourn one more time as a family and escort Tabitha's body up the hill before placing it into the cavern with her husband.

Even though their hearts were in turmoil, their sister was at peace. Korinna knew, without a grain of doubt, that Tabitha was with her heavenly Father with no more sorrow or pain that permeated this world.

She slipped back onto her mattress on the floor, no need for a cover in the warmth of the evening. Dozens of stars flickered outside her window, the eyes of God blinking back at her.

Someone stepped into her room, and in the shadows, she saw Agathon beside her bed. Closing her eyes, she coiled into the mattress as if the straw might swallow her. As if no one, including Agathon, could wake her from her sleep. She'd known this night would come, but she'd thought he would wait until after the ceremony.

Her stomach clenched, the fear inside ballooning.

She wasn't prepared for this. Not yet.

Nor would she ever be ready.

Just when she'd opened her life to God, had He closed His eyes when He looked back at her?

As Agathon stood nearby, she peeked through one eye, glancing toward the window. Those stars were still watching over her. God was there.

Somehow she would have to smother her grief, her horror, and endure what she, a slave to this man, must endure. She had no choice—

"Korinna," he muttered, his voice resigned to a whispered plea.

She hesitated before rising slowly, her back pressed against the wall as she waited for him to speak again.

He stepped toward the window, blocking the starlight as he gazed outside. Then he turned back to her. "Do you want to marry me?"

Her mouth gaped open. She'd served in this man's household for more than ten years and not once had he consulted her about even the smallest detail. And now this? No one except Tabitha had asked what she thought about this marriage, and she'd answered her friend honestly. But an honest answer to Agathon could result in a slap across her cheek.

"It's not a matter of want," she finally said, bracing herself for the pain.

Instead Agathon simply nodded. "It's a marriage of duty."

Of course it was a marriage of duty. Had he thought she might care for him? He certainly had done nothing to show that he might care for her beyond ensuring that she was fed and clothed for his service.

Perhaps a slave was supposed to adore her husband no matter how the man treated her. Was she supposed to lie in her answers? Agathon, she had no doubt, would teach her swiftly all that she was supposed to learn.

"I want you to be honest with me, Korinna." He took another step toward her. "Do you desire this marriage?"

She begged God quietly for strength. "I will do whatever is required of me."

"But you don't want to marry."

She must speak the truth now, no matter how difficult. No matter what he might do in return.

"No," she whispered, her entire body tensed to ward off the repercussions of this truth.

He leaned his ear toward her. "What did you say?"

"I don't want to marry you." Strength climbed inside her with every word. Even if he slapped her, locked her away for her impertinence, she needed to be honest with him.

"Not even for the protection it would offer?"

"Not even for that."

He slid onto the stone floor since she had no chair. "What do you want?"

Was this some sort of trick, these questions? A game that he was playing with her? But he seemed sincere, and her shoulders relaxed, ever so slightly, still prepared to absorb his rage.

"Korinna?" he prodded.

She took a deep breath and then spoke again. "I want to keep the baby that Tabitha found."

"Even with no husband…"

"I know it's impossible." No slave could care for a baby that wasn't her own. A slave who couldn't even care for herself without a master to provide for her needs. "But it's what I desire."

His hands resting on his belly, he leaned back against the wall. "I was the one who killed Tabitha. I didn't mean to, but I forced that baby on her and she…"

Her stomach rolled, but she had no response. No power to absolve him.

He closed his eyes. "What am I to do now?"

"Only the God of Tabitha can forgive you."

He ignored her offering, focusing back on their marriage. "I promised Selene that I would find you a husband."

The only man who she would dare to want, the only one she would willingly marry, was the man who deserted her master.

"And you could find none willing...."

"I haven't searched," he said. "I kept you for myself."

"You bought me, Agathon," she said, daring to use his name. "You can do with me what you wish."

"I wish—" He stood up quickly as if driven by a gale. "I know what I want."

Then he left her room, and she, with the stars still twinkling above her bed, leaned back against the wall in wonder.

The first rays of daylight were dancing between the olive leaves when Matthias woke. They'd arrived here after dark, too late to traverse the rocky path into the city, but within the hour, he and his two companions would finish this journey.

After they'd washed in the stream, Simon passed around dried figs from his pouch and Peter reached for both of their hands. He offered up a prayer of thankfulness before asking that God's will be done.

"It's time to finish our trip," Peter said, eyeing the light as it poured like oil across the dry ground.

The three men stepped out of the protection of the olive grove, and below was the tumble of Joppa's homes. The crown of this port city was a mountain of trash ahead that steamed as if it were a cauldron of stew.

When Matthias traveled to Jerusalem, he always took the well-traveled road that led around this dump, but today Peter was leading them straight toward the rubble. The narrow path was the shortest way to Joppa, but few of the villagers ever took it, except his mother.

His thoughts began to unravel like the threads of a seam, the flying pieces making his head spin. He'd been rescued from this pile long ago, but sometimes the garbage, the stench of this place, still seemed to cling to him.

While his parents had left him, God hadn't abandoned him. He sent Tabitha to love him, and now it was his turn to love those God brought his way. Scrub away the stench and do something good with his life.

"Matthias?" Simon said, traipsing up beside him.

Peter walked ahead, seeming to ignore the rancid smell that had attached itself to the wind. Perhaps the apostle knew that the men needed to speak more than the words necessary to further their journey.

Simon placed his hand on Matthias's shoulder. "What is it, Son?"

Matthias shook him away. "I'm not your son."

In the wash of ocean below, he could see Agathon's ship, and sorrow rippled through him anew at all he'd lost.

Simon glanced down at the ship. "You wronged my daughter, Matthias, but looking back, I would have done things much differently."

Matthias couldn't speak.

"In my fear, I shut you out instead of giving you an opportunity to step back into the love of Christ," Simon said. "Will you forgive me for treating you like a fugitive instead of a brother?"

Forgive him? The words stunned Matthias.

Then they shattered him.

He had been the one who'd ruined his daughter's wedding. The one who'd threatened Joshua in front of their wedding guests and then accosted Bethany in the market.

"I have hurt your entire family," Matthias said. "I'm the one who needs to beg your forgiveness."

Simon kissed his cheeks as they stood beside that pile of trash, both of them offering the other a gift. And what had been taken away from Matthias long ago seemed to be restored in that moment.

He might never know the name of the woman who birthed him, but God had given him a family. From now on, he would treat Bethany and Joshua as a sister and brother instead of a lover and an enemy.

He didn't have to fight anymore.

The men rushed to catch up with Peter, and as they began their descent into Joppa, they could hear wailing rise up from the city.

Matthias prayed again as they hiked down the rocky incline, begging God who had defeated death before to defeat it one more time.

# CHAPTER TWENTY-FIVE

The upper room was packed with dozens of women whom Tabitha had befriended over the years. Korinna, like most of them, had arrived in the hour before sunrise to say goodbye one last time to this beautiful, broken sister who'd loved with her whole heart and with the labor of her hands. With her back pressed against the summer wall, Korinna wept.

Wind gusted over the parapet, and as the sun began to rise, Glykera elbowed her way through the crowd. She deposited Hermione into Korinna's willing arms, and the baby seemed mesmerized by the wailing around them, too intrigued to cry herself.

Ianthe moved in beside her. "Tabitha wouldn't have wanted anyone mourning over her body."

"Perhaps not," Korinna said, wiping her own tears with her hand, "but we can't stop our grief."

Korinna was grieving for the loss of Tabitha, but she was also sad that Matthias was missing his mother's funeral. The community had no choice but to move ahead with the burial this morning—not even the perfume the women brought could cover the odor that had begun to seep outside this make-shift room, wafting down to the street below. They needed to honor this woman they loved by remembering the sweetness of her life, not this stench.

An empty pallet rested on the floor beside the bed for Tabitha's body, ready for Joshua to lead the pallbearers and their entire community up the hill.

Ianthe bumped against Korinna as someone else crammed into the room. All Korinna could see now was a circle of shoulders around the bed, but she feared the arrival of any more visitors might push someone over the parapet, down into the street. Or topple the remaining walls made of leaves and sticks.

A man stepped up on the pallet, and the wailing began to subside as the women studied this newcomer who dared trespass on the bier that would transport Tabitha to her grave.

"My name is Peter," the visitor announced. "I am a servant of Jesus of Nazareth."

The room grew completely silent, everyone staring at the man. Korinna rose up on her toes, searching for Matthias or Simon in the crowd. She didn't see the men, but she whispered a prayer of thankfulness that this apostle had come. He would offer hope for all of them who grieved.

"Why do you mourn?" he asked the group.

Silence was the only answer until Zoe stepped forward. "We've lost a woman that we loved as a dear sister and disciple of Jesus."

"But you cry as if you have no hope," he said. "Is Tabitha not with our Lord?"

"She is with our Lord and we're glad of it," Zoe explained, "but we've been told that even Jesus cried when He lost a dear friend. Our sorrow, I think, is equal to His."

Peter smiled as if her knowledge of his Master pleased him.

Zoe's voice grew bolder. "Like Lazarus, her work here is not done."

"What work is it that can't be done by another?" Peter asked them.

Ianthe pushed past Korinna and the others in the crowd and dropped to her knees in front of the apostle. The mourners watched quietly as she showed this man the sleeves of her garment as if they branched from a royal gown. "Tabitha made this for me, but it's more than just a tunic," Ianthe said. "She gave me a glimpse of your Lord when she shared this gift."

Miriam stepped up on the pallet, holding out the light blue skirt of her robe so Peter could see. "I was too ashamed to be seen during the daylight until Tabitha blessed me with the gift of life. She gave me a tunic and taught me to sew and now—" Her voice broke. "I'm clothed every day in her love and grace. A reminder of who I am in Christ."

Matthias stepped into the room, his face covered with dark stubble from his journey, but he carried a new confidence in his shoulders. Instead of looking down at the wrapped body laid out on the bed, he lifted his arm so that the entire room could see what he'd draped over it—a mound of brightly colored tunics.

Matthias bent over and placed the tunics on the pallet beside Peter, and then Glykera pressed through the room, adding more of these stored garments to the stack.

Matthias faced the apostle. "Her love is boundless."

Peter glanced around the room as if he was trying to understand what remained a mystery to him. "Why do so many in Joppa still not believe?"

Zoe answered him. "They don't understand as we do that God loves us even when we don't receive a miracle like others have across Judea."

Peter looked back down at the mound of clothing that Tabitha had sewn, all to be given away, before turning back to Zoe. "You will be blessed, my daughter, far beyond what you can imagine."

She smiled through her tears. "I'm already blessed."

"Joshua is waiting to begin the funeral procession," Glykera told Matthias. "But he can't find enough space to fit into this room."

The morning sun seemed to ricochet from Peter's eyes, the light blazing across all of them. "I need to be alone."

No one moved.

"Alone in this room," he said.

The crowd turned to Matthias, wondering if he would approve.

A fire seemed to sizzle inside Matthias as he lifted his arms, waving at the crowd. Then his words bellowed across the rooftops of Joppa. "Everyone out!"

All the women, except Korinna, shuffled away quickly. She couldn't seem to move as she watched Peter drop to his knees beside Tabitha, his arms lifted to the heavens as if to catch whatever God rained down on him.

And Korinna wanted it to pour down on all of them.

Peter turned to her and nodded toward the exit. She finally trailed the others down the steps, leaving this apostle alone with the body of a woman who now rested with their Lord.

"Tabitha, stand up."

This command—a muted sound from the distance—broke through the light in her mind, but she didn't want to move from this lovely place. A million threads of color dangled in soft light, all of them waiting for her needle to stitch together the most beautiful garment she'd ever created. A tapestry of warm colors. A song.

A voice spoke again, words she couldn't understand.

Had she been asleep? She must have been dreaming.

The voice beckoned her away from the beauty, back to the darkness of sleep, but she couldn't seem to move, not to open her eyes or shift her arms or legs. Not to tell him that she heard.

Why must she stand when she wanted to settle into this dream forever?

A man had been beside her, only moments ago, dressed in the most exquisite gown of white silk and golden threads. In His gaze, in the hand that had reached out for hers, she felt the love of her Father. And she'd known, deep within her, that she was cherished for exactly who He'd created her to be. That God wasn't angry at her for when she'd stumbled with her own anger.

In the distance—Isaac was waiting for her beyond the threads, his arms spread open. How she longed to run into those arms, tell him how she'd missed him, but the anchors had returned to her legs.

"Stand up," the man's voice repeated, louder now, saying her name again.

She didn't want to stand. Didn't want this dream to end. Finally she'd found a home where her soul belonged. A place of joy beyond what she'd ever known had erupted inside her, replacing the pain in her head and her heart. She wanted to stay right here, wrapped up in all the love she'd longed for.

She tried to speak again, to tell this man to stop calling for her, but she couldn't talk. Nor could she breathe.

Something was covering her face.

Fear replaced the peace as she struggled for air. For the life that she'd left behind.

Someone removed a weight from her mouth, and the breath she gulped filled her lungs. Air—blessed air—and an overwhelming perfume.

Choking, she blew the perfume right back out. What had Glykera added to her tea now? The pungency of these herbs alone might kill her.

Light slipped between her eyelids, but it wasn't the pure light from her dream that healed. The burning rays of this sunlight, she feared, would spark the flames again in her head.

Bedcovers tumbled off her as if someone had yanked them away, but she still didn't want to open her eyes lest the sun fire through her again.

But it was starlight that she'd seen before she fell asleep, not the sun. And Agathon—was he still here with her? Agathon and the baby she'd found.

She pressed her hands together, trying to remember. She'd been in the courtyard last, protecting the child from Agathon's outburst. She'd fallen with the baby in her arms.

Her stomach plunged with the memory as she searched her sides. What had happened to the child?

She blinked her eyes open, the sunlight rushing inside. She must have fallen unconscious, for it was morning now. And a man—about ten years her senior—stood beside a bed, a physician or a priest. She didn't recognize him, but one of his hands rested on her arm as if to offer comfort.

Perhaps the baby had died.

Scanning the room, she wondered where Glykera had gone. And why a mound of brightly colored linen was on the floor. The material was much too fine to waste on a bedcovering even if she was ill.

The man smiled down at her. "Welcome back, Tabitha."

She inched up on her elbows, blinking again in the face of this stranger. A plain sheet had been placed over her body. Where was her tunic and why was she alone, in this state, with a man?

"Are you a physician?"

"My name is Peter," he said. "Your son asked me to visit you."

She glanced across the empty room again. "Where is Matthias?"

Instead of answering, Peter sat down on the edge of the bed beside her, his gaze in earnest as if she held a secret he must unravel. "What was it like?"

"What…" Her voice faded out as she studied his face. The material that had covered her, the perfume that stifled her nose, soaked her skin, weren't meant for a person who'd fallen ill. They were intended for someone who wasn't supposed to return to this life.

The light that she had seen, the gentle hand of a kind master, the face of Isaac waiting for her. It hadn't been a dream. She had traveled beyond the walls of this world, to a harbor of sorts for those who had chosen to follow God.

"It was exquisite," she whispered, searching for the words to describe a place she could never describe in Hebrew or Greek or Latin or any other language of this world. "More beautiful than I could ever have imagined."

"I thought it would be so," he said, smiling again. "Did you see our Lord?"

"For a short time."

"One day you will return," he assured her. "And then it will be for an eternity."

Tabitha lay back down on the bed meant for someone who would never waken again, caught between these two worlds— one of heartache and one of peace. While she longed to be in the next life, so many she loved were still in this world, waiting to be healed by the One who had taken her hand.

"Why did you bring me back?" she asked, clutching the sheet close to her body.

"God brought you home, my sister. It seems that He still has plans for your life here in Joppa."

It was all true, everything that she'd learned about their Savior. He had gone before them to prepare a beautiful place. And He was as real as the sea that lapped against the shore below, His love even stronger than what she felt for her son and all those around her in this place.

"I was holding a baby when I fell—"

"The baby is safe with the others." Peter offered his hand. "Let's show them what God has done."

He lifted a tunic from the floor and turned away so she could dress. Then she took his hand and slowly stood up beside him.

No one would ever be able to take this gift away from her.

# CHAPTER TWENTY-SIX

While the community gathered in the courtyard, Matthias paced the length of the vestibule. The mourning outside had subsided into whispering, the murmur of questions as to who this stranger was and why he'd sent them all from the upper room when they needed to begin the funeral procession before the heat of this day.

Someone began to sing the psalm his mother loved, remembering both her life and death in their revision.

*All glorious is the princess in her chamber, with robes interwoven with gold…with joy and gladness she is led along as she enters the palace of the king.*

The melody swept through the corridor and flooded the chambers of this villa. As he listened again to the community's repetition, Matthias marveled at the thought of his mother entering into the palace of a heavenly King, dressed in a beautiful gown that she had woven herself to honor the One her soul had loved. The Father who had loved her in return.

Peter had made it quite clear that he had come to Joppa for one purpose—to encourage the fledlging church here. God might not breathe life back into his mother, but even if God didn't do this miracle, Matthias would trust in God's goodness and the life that awaited him beyond. He leaned against a relief on the wall, wondering what Peter was doing upstairs. The man might pray for hours, all day even, and God could still reject their plea.

But Imma was in a palace now. She was safe, her headaches gone. One day he would tell her that he loved her. While his sin, the turmoil in his heart, had almost broken him, one day all that had been turned upside down would be set back in place.

Korinna stepped through the archway. In her arms was Hermione, and in the midst of his grief, he felt the slightest glimpse of joy.

"What has happened to you?" she asked, her lips quivering as if she wasn't certain whether or not she should return his smile.

"Much has happened."

She eyed him with curiosity. "You're different—"

"God seemed to speak to me on this journey," he tried to explain, knowing how strange it must sound for him, of all people, to hear God's voice. "When we were traveling home, He showed me something I'd never seen before."

"It's because He loves you, Matthias. He has never abandoned you."

"I suppose not." He'd lost himself, but it seemed God had never lost him. Elohim knew where he'd been all along. "He forgave me for all that I've done."

Even in her shyness, Korinna smiled at him. "Forgiveness means that you are free, that's what Tabitha told me."

"I believe that's true.

"What's it like for you to be free?"

As he considered her question, Korinna held out Hermione to him. He hesitated at first, but he took the baby and looked down at her, as helpless as he had been when Imma found him. Tabitha had rescued him first, and then God had rescued him a second time.

He looked back at Korinna. "It means that I don't have to be afraid anymore."

In forgiveness, he could live as a man free from his past, free from sin, free to pursue a future without the chains that once bound him.

Free to love again.

"Matthias!" Someone shouted overhead, and his heart seemed to freeze.

Korinna nudged him toward the steps. "Hurry."

The baby still in his arms, he bolted for the staircase that clung to the edge of their house, leading to the roof above. Once he reached the top, he stepped around the parapet.

Then he stopped.

His mother was sitting—*sitting*—on her bed, laughing alongside Peter.

He couldn't seem to move. While he'd hoped beyond what he had believed that God could raise her, until this moment, he didn't really know if God had the power to defeat death in this life.

But God—the God above all—had brought her back to them.

Peter stepped away from the pallet when he saw Matthias, and Imma opened her arms wide.

He raced toward her and collapsed on his knees beside the bed, the colorful linen flattened under him.

"I'm so sorry," he said, blubbering over his words as he secured the baby to his chest.

"All is forgiven," she told him, and he wept on her shoulder, his love pouring out like rain on freshly planted seeds. A garden ready to grow.

When he moved back, Imma looked down at the baby between them. "God has plans for this girl," she said. "Just like He has plans for your life, Matthias."

He nodded. "I will do whatever He asks of me."

As her smile spread, he offered her the gift of this baby like Korinna had offered her to him, and his mother nestled Hermione close, at peace in this morning hour.

Moments later the peace was shattered by a gasp at the entrance. Korinna stood there, her mouth agape. Behind her were Zoe and several other women, all of them stunned into silence. Imma motioned them toward her and they moved slowly forward as if in a trance. Then a crowd flooded into the upper room.

Simon was there beside him, trying to speak, but his words came out fractured. Finally the man fell to his knees on the pallet, his head bowed in awe.

Then a wave seemed to hit the wall of people around Tabitha. One by one—Joshua, Niles, Zoe, and all of the women— they each collapsed to the ground.

And together they sang out in thankfulness to God.

The wondrous news of what happened spread rapidly across Joppa, streaming up and down the Mediterranean shore. The entire city, it seemed, gathered into the courtyard of Tabitha's home the next day to celebrate what God had done.

Why He'd chosen her, Tabitha didn't know, but people came from all over to stare, touch her skin, then hear Peter share the good news of what Jesus had done for both the Hebrew people and the Greek.

For her and her son.

God's renewal of her life was a testimony to His power and goodness. She was only a vessel, humbled and molded by the Maker. Every single breath to cross her lips was another testament to what only He could do. And the peace in Matthias— the resurrection of his life—was equally as extraordinary as her resurrection from the grave.

While her mind was strong, her body was still weak. Thank God, the pain from her head was gone, but—she smiled at the thought—the dying had drained her strength.

Or perhaps God wanted her to draw strength from the community that He'd given her this season instead of pouring herself out. He knew exactly what she—what their entire community—needed. And He'd answered her prayers for Matthias, in a much different way than she had ever imagined. Her resurrection had replenished them all with new life.

Zoe and Ianthe and the other Rhapsodies welcomed the hundreds of guests into her home for worship and worked with Glykera in the kitchen to make sure everyone had plenty to eat and drink. The inns in Joppa, she'd been told, were filled, so some travelers would spend the night in her courtyard.

As the villa overflowed with people, her heart overflowed as well. Korinna had taken over the care of Hermione as if the baby were her own child. According to Korinna, Agathon had traveled to Jerusalem, but he had given her permission to stay here with the others. The young woman made the journey to Diane's home six times over the course of each day to make sure Hermione was well fed.

Tabitha sat at the back of the courtyard, not wanting to draw any attention to herself as Peter spoke to the crowd. Even as guests came to marvel in this miracle, she prayed their community in Joppa would overflow with people who loved God with their entire being. That this glimpse of God would pour out in their love for others in and beyond this place as they began stitching together a new song.

David played with the chickens at her feet while Zoe worked. Joshua and Simon stood near the front of the court-yard, praying for those who'd asked.

Bethany joined the men, her foot bandaged and her smile a steady calm in the midst of the frenzy. If Matthias had taken note of Simon's daughter, he hadn't approached her. Instead he was sitting beside Korinna and Hermione on a blanket, listening to Peter's words.

Even though Tabitha wanted no sorrow in the face of all the goodness, she still felt sad. While she didn't know what Matthias felt, Korinna clearly loved him, and nothing that Tabitha could do, no amount of denarii she offered to pay, would release Korinna from the marriage to Agathon. The man despised Tabitha for the money that he had to give her with each journey, and he probably hated this God who had the audacity to raise her from the grave.

Matthias turned, and when he saw Tabitha, he left Korinna to join her on the divan. His arm around her, Tabitha rested against him, content in this place with her son. After years of praying, he had decided to follow the One who would never abandon him.

Whenever God called her back home, she would know that Matthias was following her into paradise.

Tabitha nodded toward Korinna. "Do you love her?"

"It doesn't matter how I feel."

She turned. "Please tell me the truth."

Matthias spoke slowly, as if each word was weighted with gold. "I believe so."

"Then we will pray for another miracle," she said. To transform all of them.

His eyes were still on Korinna when he spoke again. "I'm trying to be content no matter what happens."

"I'm proud of you, Matthias. You've become a man of faith and passion alike."

"God has led me to this place." He turned toward the entry. "And now it seems that He is about to do something new."

Her gaze followed his toward the archway, and she saw Agathon's daunting frame stretched across its breadth. After his outburst a week ago, he'd finally returned to her home.

She braced herself knowing that she shouldn't fear, that no matter what happened, God would take care of her.

"Tabitha." The man moved up beside her, his face pale, his hair coated with dust from his journey. "It's true. You are—"

She nodded. "Alive."

"The news has spread to Jerusalem." His hands trembled as he reached for a column to steady himself. "The last time I saw you…"

"It was a miracle," she said simply. "You'll want to meet the man who prayed for me, Agathon. He is a traveler like you."

Matthias didn't move from his seat, but Zoe's son stood up.

"Come," David said, holding out his hand. "I'll take you to him."

Agathon eyed the outstretched hand, and then he took it. Tabitha watched in wonder as this burly man allowed himself to be led by a boy, watched as Agathon fell on the ground in repentance at Peter's feet.

This man who had fought and deceived her had seen the same light she had. A miracle even greater, she thought, than her stepping back into this life.

God had made each of them whole again.

# CHAPTER TWENTY-SEVEN

The celebration lasted for weeks as Tabitha slowly returned to her position of hostess and leader of the Rhapsodies. People came to the courtyard in droves to ask about the resurrection and then worship together.

Korinna helped Tabitha and Zoe lead the sewing club that had expanded to dozens of women from across the region. She loved nothing more than sewing with these ladies and caring for Hermione. No one had spoken to her about what would happen to the baby once she married Agathon, but in the midst of it all, she tried not to worry. Since he'd approached her in the chamber, Agathon hadn't spoken to her again about the wedding.

Zoe spent her time stitching the remaining tunics of the five she'd commissioned from Agathon before he left for Greece. Although the man hadn't spoken with Korinna again about their marriage or her gown, he'd taken a personal interest in these last tunics, checking in regularly with Zoe as if he held a profound interest in the clothing of his staff.

Agathon's inquiries entertained most of the ladies, but not Korinna. While he claimed that his life had been changed, she didn't trust what this man, her master, might do.

Although a wedding had yet to be announced, she finished the embroidery on her gown. Agathon had allowed her to continue as a guest in Tabitha's home. When she wasn't transporting Hermione, her daylight hours were spent with Matthias, ordering material and organizing the growing collection of garments to sell at the market. In the evenings, she helped Tabitha choose which tunics to give away.

Her nights were spent in a chamber upstairs with Hermione at her side. During those late hours, she would often hear Matthias's steps down the corridor, returning from a visit with his mother. Some nights she longed to visit with the two of them, but she didn't want to intrude. As much as she wanted to make this family her own, longed even to be in Matthias's arms during the night, she was only here at the mercy of her master. It was foolish to estimate how long his mercy would last.

She had prepared her heart for the moment she must leave.

As the household slept, Korinna slipped out the back door so Hermione could eat at this quiet watch between sunset and dawn. Diane had informed her that the baby wouldn't need to continue night feedings much longer, but Korinna enjoyed the freedom of wandering while the city slept.

After Hermione ate, Korinna slipped back out into the warm moonlight, the entire city of Joppa aglow. Even if she went back to Tabitha's home now, she wouldn't be able to sleep in this heat. Better to cool herself and Hermione by the shore instead of returning to their chamber.

With Hermione secured at her side, she climbed between the outcropping of rocks where she and Matthias had talked weeks ago about Bethany. In this place where she'd known she would never be the same.

In the light of God's grace, her heart had opened up to love others. Tabitha. Hermione. And now she'd begun to love the man who had once determined to marry another. A man who would never be her husband.

How was she going to be faithful in her heart to Agathon when she longed to be with Matthias?

The moon mirrored itself on the midnight rippling of the sea, the silver waves rushing in over her sandals, cooling her feet. And she marveled at all that happened since Tabitha had returned to them.

The worship within their church had been renewed as the number who learned their choruses expanded. Each time Korinna worshipped, she realized that this life, even if it was one spent with Agathon, was only a temporary one. Tabitha had told her all about the world to come, the peace they'd experience for an eternity. While Korinna might spend this lifetime longing to be loved by her husband, she knew with confidence that she was loved by another. Forever.

"Do you see the *Chiron*?"

She jumped at the sound of Matthias's voice, the water splashing up the sides of her tunic. A mixture of irritation and anticipation swept through her like one of these waves.

"You startled me," she said before dropping her voice to a whisper as if she might awaken the creatures who slept among the rocks. "What are you doing here?"

He glanced out at the ocean. "Making sure that you and Hermione don't run away."

"But how did you know I was here?"

He sat down on the rock beside her. "I've been following you."

"Matthias!" Hermione squirmed at the sound, and she quieted her voice. "How often, exactly, have you been following me?"

"Every night," he said with a grin. "To make sure you returned home safely."

"That's foolish." Water sprayed up on her tunic again. "Why didn't you just walk with us?"

"Because you'd tell me I was being foolish."

"Of course I would have—"

"And I didn't want to hear you call me a fool."

His words silenced her. When had Matthias begun to care what she called him?

"I don't really think you're foolish," she said softly. "I just would have preferred you walk alongside me."

His smile was tentative. "That is what I'd prefer as well."

They sat for a moment in silence, listening to the gentle roar of the sea, knowing it could turn fierce. Yet the moonlight seemed to soothe its passion.

"You didn't answer my question," Matthias said.

She glanced over at him. "Which one?"

"Do you see the *Chiron*?"

She searched the dark surface of the sea until she saw the speck of a ship. "I see it."

"I promised Agathon months ago that I would go on one more voyage, but I broke that promise when I decided to…"

"I know, Matthias."

"He wants to buy the garments from the Rhapsodies at a price that, I believe, will please the women who made them, but only if I travel with the garments. He wants me to tell the story at every port about the woman who helped create them." He turned to her. "I'll be running *to* something this time, not away."

"Your mother must be happy at this news."

"I haven't told her yet."

Her gaze dropped back to the scattering of stones. "Are you worried about what she might say?"

"No," he said. "I was more concerned about you."

She looked over at him again, saw the passion on his face, and her heart skipped a beat. "Who else is going to keep watch over you when you walk home?"

"I'll be—"

He stopped her. "I want to purchase you, Korinna, so you no longer have to answer to him."

She trembled at the thought. "Agathon won't allow it."

"He is a new man in Christ, just like you and me."

The strange conversation that she'd had weeks ago with Agathon echoed in her mind, the questions he'd asked after Tabitha's death and then the resurrection that had changed his life. Perhaps in his newness, she dared to hope, he really had changed.

Matthias drew closer. "Will you allow me to ask?"

She contemplated his question. What if she didn't have to marry Agathon? Even if Matthias purchased her, she would still be a slave, but much better to be a slave in Matthias's home than to marry Agathon.

"I have no choice in what you ask or what my master will say."

His eyes were on her, the intensity peeling away the chaff around her heart. "But I still want your permission."

Matthias might be purchasing her to care for Hermione, but what an honor to be a nursemaid to this baby who already held her heart. If she couldn't be a wife to a man like Matthias, she would serve him and his family as best she could. She'd help Tabitha with her sewing and the hostessing during the day, and each night Matthias was home, she'd rest in knowing where he was, at least until he married.

"You may ask," she said.

Matthias smiled at her words. "Agathon, I'm told, sleeps little during the night hours."

"That's true but—" Her heart rippled again. "You're going to ask right now?"

"Of course." He offered his hand to lead her and Hermione off the rocks. "I must know before the ship leaves."

And that made sense. He needed to ensure that his mother had plenty of help while he traveled. Oh, to be loved by this man who cared fervidly for everyone around him.

"I can carry Hermione," he said, taking the weight of the child from her.

Matthias set a rapid pace for them through the narrow streets. Most people would be better approached in the morning hours, but Matthias seemed to know Agathon well enough to know that the harder negotiations were best done at night.

The savvy merchants, she'd once heard Agathon say, worked all hours to bargain and trade.

When Matthias pounded on the knocker, she stepped back from the door, but he waved her forward. "Please come with me."

A goat bleated in the distance, and she felt its cry keenly as if it were her own. A cry that knew not whether it was happy or afraid.

Instead of Laurel or another servant, Agathon opened the door. While he invited Matthias inside, he didn't say anything to Korinna. Matthias motioned for her to follow.

Agathon's lantern cast long shadows down the walls of the corridor. He led them upstairs to the private chamber where he conducted his business dealings, removing the keys from his belt before unlocking the large door.

In the past thirteen years that she'd worked in this household, Korinna had never been inside. Peering into the room, she saw a set of divans with red and golden cushions that matched the silk carpet and a stone table centered in the middle of the room, its feet carved like lion paws. She began to follow the men through the door, but this time Agathon stopped her.

"Wait outside," he said, master to slave.

Trembling, she stepped back. "Yes, my lord."

Perhaps he hadn't changed after all.

Matthias handed Hermione to her, then winked. Or, at least, it looked like he winked in the dim light. That confidence that she longed for, Matthias embodied. If only he could pass this confidence along to her.

With the baby asleep in her arms, she lowered herself to the floor, leaning back against the cool stone. The only light in the corridor loomed in a circle from the keyhole, shining a miniature moon on the dark galaxy of wall.

The men's voices spilled out of the keyhole with the light, and she inched toward it, propping her ear against the door.

Matthias was speaking, and she wished that she could see his face when he spoke to Agathon. "I want to buy Korinna from you," he said.

She held her breath in the silence, waiting for Agathon to reply. "Why do you want to buy her?"

"To redeem her," he explained. "Imma and I want her to be free."

Her breath caught in her throat as she sank back to the ground. Matthias hadn't mentioned wanting to set her free.

How she wanted this freedom, but if Agathon said yes…

Where exactly was a free, unmarried woman supposed to go?

In the freedom of her heart and her life, surely God would show her the way.

"I won't sell her," Agathon said behind the door.

Her chest quickly deflated. She'd guessed that he wouldn't allow her to leave, but she had still allowed herself to hope.

"Agathon—" Matthias's voice grew in strength, blasting through the wooden barrier.

"I won't sell her, but I'll give her to you under one condition."

A long silence followed before Matthias responded. "What condition?"

Korinna pressed her ear to the door, but the men had lowered their voices. Whatever the condition, she feared Matthias would run again, and she couldn't blame him. Agathon would still be ruthless in his transactions of business even if he was changed in his heart.

The men continued talking, but all she heard was the low rumble of words. Words that meant everything to her, she couldn't understand.

Her eyes began to weigh heavy. As she waited, she retucked the cloth around Hermione and gently lowered her to the floor. Then, with her hand on the baby, she succumbed to sleep.

Minutes passed, hours even, before Matthias awakened her.

"Korinna," he whispered, shaking her arm. "It's time to go home."

But here was her home, with Agathon. Even if she spent another night in Tabitha's house, it would never be hers. Why return to a place she didn't belong? Here, at least, she knew what to expect. Knew, without any doubt, that she would never be free.

"I can't bear to go back, Matthias." He wouldn't understand. He had done his best to redeem her, but not even he could overcome what Agathon had planned.

He sat down beside her, crossing his legs. "Why can't you bear it?"

"Because I don't belong in your home. If Agathon won't let you buy me, I need to stay here."

"Oh, Korinna…"

"I can't—"

He hushed her, his finger on her lips. "Agathon wouldn't sell you because he gave you to me."

She reached for his hand and lowered it from her flushed skin. "I don't understand."

"He offered us a dowry, if you'll have me."

Her head began to spin, and she wondered if she was dreaming. A dowry—only brides were given a dowry. Cherished brides with fathers who found them a caring husband. No one, especially not Agathon, would give her away with such a gift.

She lifted Hermione from the ground, held her close as if she were a shield for her heart. While she understood his words, they couldn't possibly be true.

"Will you marry me?" Matthias asked. "You will be free, whether or not we marry, but if you'll have me, I would like nothing more than for you to be my wife and for Hermione to be our daughter."

"But Bethany—"

He stopped her. "I love *you*, Korinna."

She started to protest again, but he pulled her closer to him. "God has redeemed both of us."

Her breath caught in wonder, words buried somewhere deep inside. He was leaving soon on the ship, but if he really returned to Joppa, if they could marry, it was far more than she ever imagined for her life. The redemption had spilled over from her heart, breaking through the chains of her life.

He spoke faster. "I want to serve Him alongside you, but only if you want it. You can marry someone else if you choose."

And she realized that he was nervous. Worried, even, that she might say no.

"Matthias…" Her heart beat faster. "There's nothing I want more than to be with you."

# CHAPTER TWENTY-EIGHT

The *Chiron* returned the first of November, and the moment they dropped anchor, Matthias boarded the first lighter headed to Joppa's shore. Imma greeted him in the harbor, her arms strong once again, her smile welcoming him in the drizzling rain.

"You'll catch cold," he said, alarmed that she'd wait for him in this miserable weather.

"I had to greet my son."

He removed his leather coat and draped it over her shoulders. She'd loved him well for twenty years, and he'd spent every day on the ship grateful for her love and her life.

Over the past months, he'd been faithful to share her story at every port he'd visited, but even as he shared and sold the garments made by the Rhapsodies, he longed only to be home.

He glanced across the small crowd, yearning to see the woman his heart longed for, hoping that Korinna had missed him too.

"She's waiting for you at home," Imma said. "She wanted to greet you in private."

He smiled, wanting nothing more than to greet her in return. "And Hermione?"

"She is well and eager to see her father."

The word rang like a welcome chime in his ears. Here he had an entire family waiting.

As they walked, he told her about his journey. While he didn't know how many believed this resurrection story, the crowds had listened. Other men and women, he hoped, would come after him to share their own stories of how God had worked a miracle.

And he'd been on a mission of his own during this trip. After he shared Imma's miracle, after all the garments had been bartered and sold, he'd searched each port for the finest rugs and furnishings, acquiring the brightest colors possible so his bride would remember always that she was loved. The two hundred denarii that Agathon insisted upon as a dowry was used for her good.

Korinna had told him once that he needed to stop running, but this morning he wanted to run again, as quickly as possible, to her.

He rushed into the villa, but neither Korinna nor Hermione was waiting for him there. Glykera refused to tell him where they went, and he tried not to worry as he rapidly washed in the bath that Glykera insisted he take. Then he dressed and shaved in minutes, the fears returning that Korinna had changed her mind.

Had she abandoned him while he was gone? Perhaps Glykera and Imma were afraid to tell him. Korinna was free now to marry whomever she chose, or she could leave Joppa if she wanted. The choice was hers, and while he'd tried to fight against his own doubts, he was keenly aware that she might not choose him.

And if she didn't, he would have to let her go.

"Where is Korinna?" he asked again, his heart pounding when he stepped back into the kitchen.

Imma, dressed in an elegant garment of pearl and green, took his arm. Instead of answering, she smiled at him. "Come with us."

The rain had stopped, the drops glistening in the afternoon sun as Imma led him and Glykera down the street, to Agathon's villa. While part of him feared that something happened to the woman who'd promised to marry him, his mother wasn't the least bit somber. It would have broken her heart if Korinna left them.

Perhaps they were surprising him with a feast to welcome him home.

But, if so, why weren't they having a feast at their villa?

Imma knocked on Agathon's door, and they waited for Laurel to answer it. The last time he'd been in this house, Agathon had agreed to let him wed Korinna. Matthias refused the dowry at first, but Agathon insisted, saying he wanted to bring honor to Selene and the girl he'd refused to adopt.

The money Matthias hadn't spent on furnishings, he planned to save for Hermione. Perhaps he would use it toward a dowry when it was time for her to marry.

After Laurel opened the door, Imma took his arm again and guided him through the vestibule. The courtyard was filled with people standing under the palm trees, and when he arrived, the crowd parted.

Like fog lifting from a dream, sudden clarity woke him from his daze.

Before him was the woman he loved, clothed in a tunic that reminded him of the violet waters surrounding Cyprus at daybreak, its sleeves embroidered with flowers in a garden of shades. Woven through her dark hair were the white and purple buds of saffron and the light in her eyes glistened like stars.

Her smile spread gently across her lips, and in that moment, he knew this was much more than a party to welcome him home. It was a wedding feast.

His bride had faith that God would bring him home. And she had faith that he wouldn't run this time. Korinna had waited, making him the most blessed man in this world.

Agathon was in the crowd, sitting on a divan between Zoe and David. The man nodded at Matthias, the approval of a father giving away his daughter instead of a man about to lose his potential wife.

Matthias stood beside Korinna, in awe as Simon prayed for their union. Then Glykera handed him the baby, who had grown in the months he'd been traveling. Hermione's eyes were the color of Korinna's tunic, and they studied him closely before her hand reached out to find his chin.

No matter what they faced as a family, he would never abandon this girl.

With Hermione in one arm, he reached for the hand of his wife, and they moved back under the canopy of a tree. Imma and Bethany led the group in both prayer and song as they worshipped together in the midst of the celebration.

Korinna reached for the hand that he'd hidden under his sleeve, and she brushed her fingers over the tips of his, stopping at the nub where he should have had a thumb. Slowly she lifted his hand and then she leaned over and kissed his skin, not alarmed by what he'd lost.

"You don't need to hide this anymore," she whispered.

While the courtyard swayed under his legs, a reminder from his weeks on the sea, his heart was anchored firmly with the woman beside him. And he turned toward the feast that the Rhapsodies prepared for this day.

Rolling up his sleeve, he forgot about the missing thumb until later that day when Ianthe approached him, a bouquet of lilies ready to give to his bride. But instead of speaking with Korinna, she was looking down at his left hand as if it were a claw, her eyes enlarged like the fullness of the moon.

He pulled it back one more time under his sleeve in a reprisal of shame.

"No," she said softly, pulling it out again. "It's a gift."

Confused, he looked at Korinna, but she simply shrugged, smiling at the woman who only wanted to help.

"How could it be a gift?" he asked.

"Because you're marked like no other."

Korinna stepped forward, taking the lilies from her. "Thank you for the flowers."

But Ianthe's eyes were still on him, filling up with tears.

"Is something the matter?" he asked.

"No." She enclosed his broken hand in hers. Then she closed her eyes for a moment and muttered something to herself. "All is well, Son."

He leaned down and kissed her forehead before turning back to his bride.

The older woman was right. All was well.

No matter what happened in this world, another world awaited them beyond. And this love between those gathered here reflected the eternal love to come.

# AUTHOR'S NOTE

Writing this book was a personal journey as I researched the history of a woman who has intrigued me for years. Beyond the few verses recorded by Luke in the Book of Acts, we don't know much about the woman called Tabitha by the Jewish people and Dorcas by the Greeks. We do know her name meant *gazelle*, and she was clearly an inspiration to her entire community as a Hellenistic Jewish woman who used her gift of sewing for God's glory. Acts 9:36 tells us, "She was always doing good and helping the poor." What a beautiful tribute to this woman whose story prompted many across the region to believe in the Lord.

Luke didn't record Tabitha's reaction to her resurrection, nor do we have many key facts like when Tabitha was raised from the dead or if she was a young or older widow, mother, or woman who'd embraced singleness for life.

Beyond her sewing, how did Tabitha help the poor? Whom did she love? And what exactly did she experience when she slipped into eternity?

We're left to wonder at what must have been a remarkable life.

With great joy, my mind traveled to the beautiful port of Joppa as I wrote and imagined what Tabitha's life and death might have been like in the first century. I learned about the Jewish culture in this secular port and about those who'd become devoted disciples of Christ with their regular meetings to pray, worship, and eat as a community.

As I researched, it was fascinating to learn about the similarities between Tabitha's miracle and the resurrection of Jairus's daughter in the Gospel of Mark. Both of these resurrections were catalysts to opening the door for Gentiles like me to experience and follow Christ.

It's been a great honor to share my perspective on Tabitha's resurrection story. Thank you for joining me on this journey.

# FACTS BEHIND *the Fiction*

# HOW A PROPER JEWISH
# WOMAN DRESSED

We know what Jewish women wore in the early years of the Christian church because, amazingly, a stash of clothes from this time survived, buried in a dry cave almost 2,000 years ago with a man, woman, and child. They were found near the oasis spring of Ein Gedi alongside the Dead Sea, a little more than a day's walk south of Jerusalem.

Based on what archaeologists found, along with what they've learned from ancient paintings and written descriptions from that era, Jews in the region generally wore just two main pieces of clothing: a tunic and a cloak, or mantle. Women generally wore a long tunic with long sleeves. The cloak was often a large rectangle of wool. Wearers often draped it over a shoulder, on top of the tunic. Then they tied it under one arm, leaving the other arm free to work. In cool weather, they draped the cloak over their shoulders. At night, they could use it as a blanket or a pillow.

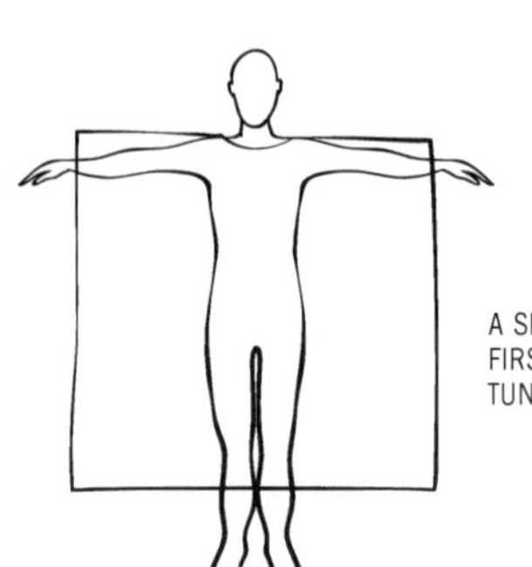

A WOMAN DRESSED IN TYPICAL FIRST-CENTURY JEWISH ATTIRE.

A SIMPLE
FIRST-CENTURY
TUNIC

# FINEST WEAVERS IN THE EMPIRE

Customers throughout the Roman Empire recognized Jewish weavers in the Holy Land as among the best at their trade. They were famous for their weaving and dyeing in Tabitha's time and beyond, so much so that one Egyptian church historian, Clement of Alexandria, complained that his fellow Egyptians weren't buying enough Egyptian fabric anymore. He said they preferred fabric imported from "the land of the Jews."

One Galilean village alone, Kfar Namra (Khirbet Amodam), a few miles from the Nazareth hometown of Jesus, boasted 300 weaving shops. Weaving flourished in many other villages throughout the area.

The Galilean town of Beth Shean supplied fabric for the entire Roman world and beyond. This Roman-styled city just south of the Sea of Galilee had a reputation for selling the world's best and highest-priced linen.

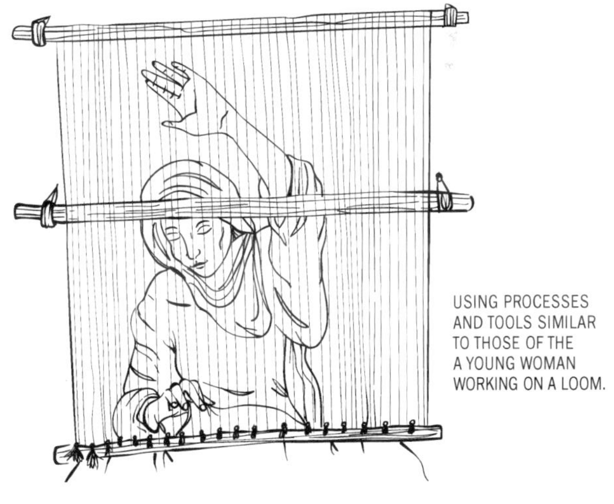

USING PROCESSES AND TOOLS SIMILAR TO THOSE OF THE A YOUNG WOMAN WORKING ON A LOOM.

## DON'T MIX LINEN AND WOOL

Moses told Jews during their exodus out of slavery in Egypt: "When you weave cloth for clothing, you can use thread made of flax or wool, but not both together" (Deuteronomy 22:11 CEV). Partly because of this rule, some Jewish shops specialized in one fabric or the other. It kept them from accidentally blending the two. Besides, it was simpler to focus on one production process.

## STEPS TO PRODUCE WOOL FABRIC

More than 1,700 pieces of fabric have survived from the 100s BC to the AD 200s, when Romans ruled. Six out of ten are wool. Most of the rest are linen. Very few are made of goat hair or the camel hair that John the Baptist wore. None are cotton.

To produce wool, the main fabric used for Jewish clothing, workers needed to:

- Shear wool from sheep or goats
- Wash and comb away the natural lanolin, oil, dirt, and plant remnants
- Dye wool, if desired
- Spin wool into yarn
- Weave yarn into cloth

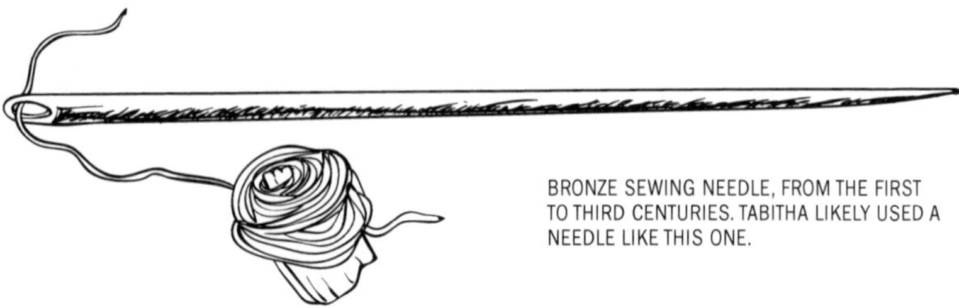

BRONZE SEWING NEEDLE, FROM THE FIRST TO THIRD CENTURIES. TABITHA LIKELY USED A NEEDLE LIKE THIS ONE.

## SEWING

The job of a seamstress in Roman times was considered respectable, though low in status. A seamstress in Tabitha's time sewed by hand, much like we sometimes do today when we use a needle and thread to repair a torn piece of clothing.

Needles have been around for thousands of years. Some of the first were slivers of bone with a tiny slit in the top, to hold the thread in place. By Tabitha's time, seamstresses were using needles made of bronze. Many survived and remain in good enough shape to use today.

The job of drilling eyes into needles small enough to hold a linen thread was the job of an artisan with an awl, a sharp tool to puncture holes into objects. This was done by hand until the early 1800s.

As is the case today, clothes got recycled down the social ladder, from riches to rags. Some seamstresses became known as patch-workers because they pieced together clothes from recycled scraps of cloth.

## PETER: LIFE AFTER JESUS

Peter was known as a talker before he saw Jesus come back from the dead. Bible writers portray him as a spokesman for the dozen disciples, taking their toughest questions to Jesus. But once Peter saw the resurrected Jesus, his outspokenness increased over the next thirty-some years. His words literally became the death of him.

Peter first risked his life a few weeks after the resurrection. He preached a sermon that jump-started the Christian movement. He did that in Jerusalem, right in front of the Jewish leaders who had orchestrated the execution of Jesus—perhaps just a few hundred yards away.

Peter told the crowd that swarmed into the city for the early harvest festival of Pentecost

A STATUE OF APOSTLE PETER STANDS OUTSIDE THE BASILICA OF SAINT PETER IN ROME. CHURCH TRADITION IDENTIFIES PETER AS THE FIRST POPE.

that Jesus was alive. "Those who believed what Peter said were baptized and added to the church that day—about 3,000 in all" (Acts 2:41 NLT).

Peter was later arrested in the city but escaped. His close friend and former fellow fisherman, James, the first apostle to be martyred for Jesus, was executed by Herod Agrippa, grandson of King Herod the Great, who had tried to kill the baby Jesus in Bethlehem.

Peter and Paul had at least one run-in. Paul accused Peter of favoring Jewish believers over non-Jewish ones: "What he did was very wrong" (Galatians 2:11 NLT). The clash seemed short-lived. Near the end of Peter's life, he wrote at least one letter to believers in what is now Turkey, where Paul started churches on his three mission trips.

Early church writers say the Romans executed both Peter and Paul in Rome. They died around the time Emperor Nero launched the first persecution of Christians. He blamed Christians for starting the fire that burned most of Rome in the summer of AD 64.

Peter reportedly died crucified upside down. Paul, as a Roman citizen, had the legal right to a speedy execution. Early church leaders say he was beheaded.

## HOW JEWS MOURNED THE DEAD

Jews generally practiced same-day burial. That's because they didn't embalm, and the weather was hot most of the year.

Moses didn't give the Jews laws about how to mourn the dead. But Jews and others throughout the ancient Middle East commonly practiced mourning traditions such as:

- wearing torn clothes
- putting ashes on their heads
- mourning with others for seven days before shifting back into the routines of life.

Just as preachers today often advise people how to deal with tough times, rabbis did the same for Jews. Some rabbis offered the following rules for mourning:

- Don't wear new clothes, even on the Sabbath.
- Don't wash yourself or your clothes during the week of mourning.
- Limit the most intense mourning to the first day or two, and then find comfort for your sorrow.
- Don't work. That includes preparing meals. Eat only food others bring you.

One rabbi said people should mourn at least a day or two "to avoid criticism." Another rabbi said that even the poorest person in Israel should hire at least "one wailing woman" and two musicians to play flutes.

# WHY JEWS ADOPTED CHILDREN

For Romans as well as Jews, the most common reason people in Bible times adopted a child was because they didn't have one.

Children were heirs as well as a form of social security. In a day before government-funded programs to help the poor and the elderly, grown children maintained the family property, took care of their aging parents, buried them when they died, mourned them, and preserved the family name.

Some adopted a child because they needed an apprentice to help with a business and carry on with the work when the adoptive parents couldn't work anymore.

A DEPICTION OF A FIRST-CENTURY JEWISH FAMILY, ADAPTED FROM AN ANCIENT RELIEF

For Jews, the child's biological family—not the adoptive family—determined the status of the child. In terms of status, for example, the son of a Jewish slave adopted out of slavery remained the son of a slave, even though he inherited from his adopted family.

For Romans, it was different. An adopted son also inherited the social status of his new family, whether it was a step up to the ruling class of patrician or a step down to a common citizen, "plebeian."

Roman and Jewish couples alike preferred to adopt the oldest son in a family. It was more expensive to adopt firstborn sons than girls or other sons if adopted out of someone else's established family.

Some very poor families might offer their son for adoption for money that would help the rest of the family survive. Some families saw an opportunity for their child to move up in life to better circumstances, or perhaps to learn a trade.

## JOPPA, CITY BY THE SEA

Joppa was a seaside village in a nation of Jewish herders and farmers more sea-fearing than seafaring. In addition to the story of Tabitha, the city is mentioned in the Bible because of three notable characters.

Solomon. When King Solomon built the first Jewish Temple, he ordered cedar lumber from Lebanon. Lebanon's king arranged to "make them into rafts and float them along the coast" (1 Kings 5:9 NLT). Then he had them brought ashore at Joppa's port and hauled 40 miles (65 km) to Jerusalem.

Jonah. God ordered the prophet Jonah to go to the Assyrians, fierce warriors in what is now Iraq, and condemn them as an evil empire. Jonah went to Joppa and caught a ship headed "in the opposite direction" (Jonah 1:3 NLT).

Peter. It was on the rooftop at a tanner's house in Joppa that Peter

MOSAIC OF A GAZELLE FROM ROMAN TIMES IN CAESAREA, ISRAEL. THE NAME TABITHA (DORCAS) MEANTING "GAZELLE."

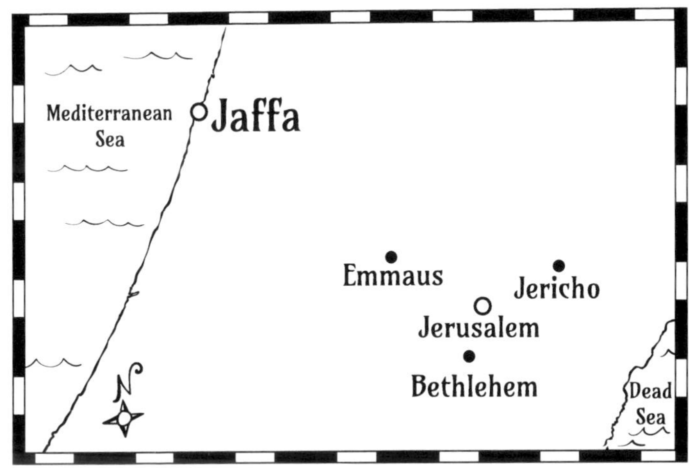



JOPPA (NOW CALLED JAFFA) IS LOCATED ON THE MEDITERRANEAN SHORE OF ISRAEL, APPROXI-MATELY 40 MILES (65 KM) FROM JERUSALEM.

had a remarkable vision of God telling him to eat non-kosher food. Three times God provided animals that Jews were forbidden to eat and directed Peter to kill them and eat them. Three times Peter refused to defile himself by eating "unclean" food. And three times God told him, "Do not call something unclean if God has made it clean" (Acts 10:15 NLT). While Peter was still puzzling over what this vision could possibly mean, the Holy Spirit told him, "Three men have come looking for you. Get up, go downstairs, and go with them without hesitation. Don't worry, for I have sent them" (verses 19–20).

Sure enough, when Peter went downstairs, there were three men waiting for him. They took Peter to see Cornelius, an officer in the Roman army, who told him a remarkable story of how an angel of God had appeared to him and told him to find Peter. Then Peter remembered his vision and knew that God was telling him that Gentiles were just as welcome as the Jews to become Christians and follow Jesus. Peter baptized Cornelius and his family and said, "I see very clearly that God shows no favoritism. In every nation he accepts those who fear him and do what is right" (Acts 10:34–35 NLT).

Fiction Author
# MELANIE DOBSON

Writing fiction is **Melanie Dobson's** excuse to explore abandoned houses, travel to unique places, and immerse herself in old journals and books. The award-winning author of almost thirty novels, Melanie enjoys stitching together both historical and time-slip stories. She has written four biblical fiction stories for Guideposts.

Five of Melanie's novels have won Carol Awards and two were finalists for a Christy Award. She is the previous corporate publicity manager at Focus on the Family and now enjoys teaching as an adjunct professor in the Pacific Northwest.

## Nonfiction Author
# STEPHEN M. MILLER

**Stephen M. Miller** is an award-winning, best-selling Christian author of easy-reading books about the Bible and Christianity. His books have sold over 1.9 million copies and include *The Complete Guide to the Bible, Who's Who and Where's Where in the Bible,* and *How to Get into the Bible.*

Miller lives in the suburbs of Kansas City with his wife, Linda, a registered nurse. They have two married children who live nearby.

# RICH BEYOND MEASURE:
# ZLATA'S STORY

## by Robin Lee Hatcher

**Z**lata. Zlata, you are needed. Come now."

Zlata groaned, trying to refuse the summons by sheer will.

Dara shook her shoulder. "Now, Zlata. The mistress needs you."

She opened her eyes at last. The room was dark except for the flickering light provided by the lamp the young servant carried. Zlata wondered how long she had been asleep. Ten minutes. An hour. However much, it had been too little.

"I'm coming, Dara." She shoved aside the light covering on her sleeping mat and sat up, hair tumbling over her shoulders as she leaned forward in search of her sandals.

Her mother-in-law's illness had cast a pall over the household for several weeks. With Abra too sick to travel to Jerusalem for Passover, Zlata's father-in-law, Taneli, had gone alone. He wasn't a patient or kind man under the best circumstances, and his wife's failing health had made him even surlier. Since his return to Capernaum, he'd spent little time at home. But that was not unusual. His obligations took him to the synagogue daily. He was an important man in the region.

It was just as well for Zlata that Taneli was wanted elsewhere for most hours of the day. He believed all women were beneath him, but he particularly detested the sight of his daughter-in-law. She understood. She reminded him of Yerik, his only son. Taneli blamed her for Yerik's death. So she did her best to remain unnoticed, a ghost within the walls of this household. But how would she avoid him in the middle of the night?

After hastily making herself presentable, she followed Dara from the room. They found Abra alone in the large sleeping chamber on the opposite side of the house, rolling her head from side to side, face beaded with sweat. She mumbled nonsensical words in a continuous stream.

Zlata knelt at the edge of the bed and took her mother-in-law's hand. Leaning close, she said, "I am here, Abra."

Her mother-in-law's fingers tightened, ever so slightly, around Zlata's hand. The two of them were not close. Like her husband, Abra scarcely gave Zlata notice. But still the woman must have drawn some comfort from her care.

Dara brought a bowl of water and a clean cloth to the bedside, and Zlata used it to cool Abra's forehead. Softly, she whispered the words of David, "'In peace I will both lie down and sleep; for You alone, O Lord, make me dwell in safety.'" She leaned closer. "My lady, the Lord causes you to dwell in safety. You may rest now."

Her own chest tightened as she spoke the words. They were the same ones her father had said to her mother when she lay dying. Zlata had watched from the opposite side of the bed as he'd tenderly ministered to his wife, and she'd thanked God for blessing her with devoted parents and a good, God-fearing home. By their example, she had learned what a loving marriage should look like.

Zlata had believed that her mother's death was the worst that could happen to her. How naive she'd been. How foolish. Her mother's death had not been the worst. It had only been the beginning of Zlata's losses, one piled upon another.

Zlata had been a favored child, loved and cherished by her parents. If her father had grieved over not having a son, he'd never once shown those feelings to his daughter. Instead he'd called her the apple of his eye, and she'd believed him. A fisherman by trade, her father had never had much money, but he'd known how to care for his family. Most important to him was to raise his daughter to love the God of Israel. Of next importance had been to find Zlata a good and caring husband. He had succeeded on both counts.

When Zlata left her girlhood home on her wedding day—eleven years ago this month—she'd seen tenderness in the eyes of her waiting bridegroom. The look had calmed the fear of the sixteen-year-old girl she'd been. Her nerves had been chased away by his handsome smile. When Yerik promised to care for her always, she'd believed him. She'd learned to love him in the time they had together. Time that had been all too brief. Less than three years.

In those same three years, death swallowed her mother, her father, and her husband. And then, it had come for—

She squeezed her eyes shut, pushing away the memories and stopping the final one from taking their place.

This was her life. Living in the home of her in-laws, caring for their needs. Without the inheritance of her bride price from her father—money he'd spent in his desperate attempt to save her mother's life—Zlata had been left with nothing. Taneli and Abra could have cast her out. She might have starved to death long before this or been forced into an unspeakable way of life in order to survive. The thought terrified her, as so many things did. She should be grateful that she had not fallen into such circumstances. She *was* grateful. Yet she couldn't pretend it wasn't hard. Loneliness overwhelmed her at times. She felt invisible, afraid, forgotten, and her heart had been hardened by bitterness.

Dara's fingertips touched Zlata's shoulder. "The mistress sleeps."

Zlata looked and saw that it was true. Usually Abra's bad spells lasted much longer. Relieved for the change, she stood. "Then we should sleep too."

Dara nodded.

"I will see you in the morning."

Zlata didn't wait for confirmation from the young servant nor did she take the candle the girl offered. She knew the placement of each room and the location of every piece of furniture in them. She could make her way through the house without trouble, even on the darkest of nights. Still, when she stepped out of the bedchamber, she was afraid she might stumble into her father-in-law in the dark. But she didn't, and soon enough she was lying on the mat in her own small room.

Sleep refused to come again. Instead her thoughts whirled backward in time, back to those few precious years with Yerik, back to when she'd discovered a new life was blossoming within her. For a time—for such a brief time—this had been a house filled with rejoicing. She'd known the love of her husband. She'd known the approval of her mother-in-law. Even Taneli had smiled upon her, for she was doing what God had intended her to do. She'd seen the years stretching before her in contented bliss. Yerik tending the family vineyards. Taneli teaching in the synagogue. Zlata, with the help of Abra, raising Yerik's children as they came along. Her heart had been full. Even the deaths of her parents hadn't completely marred her joy.

Bitterness rose like bile. How could God have allowed everything to go so wrong? Why had He taken her mother, her father, her husband, and finally her infant son? What sin had she committed to deserve such punishment?

Rolling onto her side, she allowed tears to wet her pillow. Weeping changed nothing, of course. In the morning she would still rise alone, as always. She would still be afraid. And the years that stretched before her would still be filled with sorrow.

The following day, Taneli's raised voice reached Zlata in the courtyard. Her father-in-law and his close friend, Nathan the younger, had been debating points of the law for much of the morning, but now they had turned their attention upon a man called Yeshua the Nazarene. Zlata had heard of the teacher. Who in Capernaum didn't know his name? He was often mentioned by other women in the marketplace and at the well. Many miracles were attributed to him. It was rumored that Yeshua had cured a demoniac the previous year. She remembered her father-in-law's reaction when he'd heard that this so-called healing had happened on the Sabbath.

Taneli was a righteous and learned man, a Pharisee, a man in authority at the synagogue in Capernaum. He was outraged that Yeshua, who had begun attracting larger crowds in recent months, would perform any kind of work on the Sabbath. A sure sign that he was not a prophet, as some had declared him to be. Yeshua was a charlatan, a nobody. Taneli didn't understand why the rabbi from Nazareth was allowed to teach in the synagogues throughout Galilee. Her father-in-law, try as he might, hadn't been able to stop it in Capernaum either.

Hearing the increasing rage in her father-in-law's voice, Zlata decided to make herself scarce lest he vent some of that anger in her direction. She hurried to gather the clothes for washing, then left through the courtyard doorway.

The house of Taneli had many rooms that surrounded a fine courtyard. Its size proclaimed the success of the family vineyards to anyone who passed by. Built on a hillside, it had a fine view of the Sea of Galilee, especially from the rooftop. Oh, how Yerik had loved to stand on that rooftop and look out over the lake. He'd loved the water when the sky was clear and sunlight danced upon the glassy surface like a thousand stars. He'd loved it when storms blew through, the skies gray and the lake churning. Although her husband's work had been tied to the vineyards, his heart had leaned toward the Sea of Galilee.

Dear, sweet Yerik. She hadn't liked the idea of marriage when she was fifteen and first learned of the betrothal her father had arranged. Yerik had been a stranger to her. But in time, he'd won her heart with his kindness and with his laughter. His simple joy, his love of life, had infected everyone around him. Even Taneli had been different when with his son.

Zlata hardened her heart against the sweet memories. Better to beat back the rising emotions while she laundered the clothes. Better to let her tears mix with the wash water and soak into the earth, unseen. Like Zlata herself.

# A NOTE FROM THE EDITORS

We hope you enjoyed another volume in the Ordinary Women of the Bible series, created by Guideposts. For over seventy-five years, Guideposts, a nonprofit organization, has been driven by a vision of a world filled with hope. We aspire to be the voice of a trusted friend, a friend who makes you feel more hopeful and connected.

By making a purchase from Guideposts, you join our community in touching millions of lives, inspiring them to believe that all things are possible through faith, hope, and prayer. Your continued support allows us to provide uplifting resources to those in need. Whether through our communities, websites, apps, or publications, we inspire our audiences, bring them together, and comfort, uplift, entertain, and guide them. Visit us at guideposts.org to learn more.

We would love to hear from you. Write us at Guideposts, P.O. Box 5815, Harlan, Iowa 51593 or call us at (800) 932-2145. Did you love *An Eternal Love: Abigal's Story*? Leave a review for this product on guideposts.org/shop. Your feedback helps others in our community find relevant products.

# Find more inspiring stories in these best-loved Guideposts fiction series!

## Mysteries of Lancaster County

Follow the Classen sisters as they unravel clues and uncover hidden secrets in Mysteries of Lancaster County. As you get to know these women and their friends, you'll see how God brings each of them together for a fresh start in life.

## Secrets of Wayfarers Inn

Retired schoolteachers find themselves owners of an old warehouse-turned-inn that is filled with hidden passages, buried secrets, and stunning surprises that will set them on a course to puzzling mysteries from the Underground Railroad.

## Tearoom Mysteries Series

Mix one stately Victorian home, a charming lakeside town in Maine, and two adventurous cousins with a passion for tea and hospitality. Add a large scoop of intriguing mystery, and sprinkle generously with faith, family, and friends, and you have the recipe for *Tearoom Mysteries*.

## Mysteries of Martha's Vineyard

Come to the shores of this quaint and historic island and dig in to a cozy mystery. When a recent widow inherits a lighthouse just off the coast of Massachusetts, she finds exciting adventures, new friends, and renewed hope.

### To learn more about these books, visit Guideposts.org/Shop

Printed in the United States
by Baker & Taylor Publisher Services